OFFSIDE

A VANCOUVER VIKINGS HOCKEY ROMANCE

SIERRA HILL

TEN28 PUBLISHING

or go to

BookFunnel download:

https://BookHip.com/LBWFHAP

ENJOY!

Xoxo

Sierra

1

Ballas - June

Ah shit. There goes my contract extension.

All because my dick got in the way. I figured one day my dick would finally get me in trouble.

I stare at the beautiful woman across the table from me, flanked by the GM and the attorney for the Vikings, who are all here for the same reason. To renegotiate the terms of my contract.

What is it that they say about your past catching up to you? Or never mixing business with pleasure?

Well, unfortunately for me, my past just caught up with me and my pleasure may have just fucked up my future plans.

I guess it's time to deal with the consequences of the actions of my dick.

"Thank you for meeting with us today, gentlemen," Karis says in a quiet yet firm tone, nodding briskly at both me and my agent, Quincy Peck, who sits in the chair to my right. "I'm sure you both know Nate and our team attorney, Tarjinder Singh."

Sitting to her left is Nate McGowan, the Vikings GM, an asshole of epic proportions who I can't stand. On the other side is our team's attorney, Tarjinder, a man in his late fifties whose hair is graying at the temples. His mustache and dark eyebrows are distracting from the seriousness of this meeting because they remind me almost too much of Groucho Marx. I have to stifle a chuckle.

I stare back at the gorgeous woman who I fucked into oblivion six months ago in a hotel room in Vegas. That was the night of my best friend Marek's wedding and the night Karis Spurlock approached me in the hotel bar with a proposition I couldn't pass up.

Back then, Karis wasn't my boss's boss or the franchise owner of the Vikings. She was simply another wedding guest and the niece of Marvin Spurlock, the Vikings' team owner, and the owner of the Puget Sound Pilots' basketball team. *Marek's* boss. *Not* mine.

When Karis boldly asked for a hot, no-strings-attached hookup that night, I happily obliged. Who was I to turn down a beautiful woman?

Had I known then what I know now, would I have done it?

Fuck, that's yet to be determined.

We may have screwed each other's brains out in Vegas, but right now, Karis Spurlock could screw me in an entirely different way. She holds the key to my future on the team, or possibly the end of my NHL career.

Quincy interrupts my thoughts, dragging my attention off Karis and back to the seriousness of the situation. "Good afternoon, Ms. Spurlock, gentlemen. Ballas and I are eager to discuss the terms of the contract extension."

Karis gives a tight smile, her hand landing on the paperwork that decides whether I stay with the Vikings, get traded, or —God forbid—end up on the affiliate. A small flicker of unease settles in my bones. That third one is always an option for a veteran player like me, and last year was especially tough. Considering my eighteen years in the league, the team may want to bring in younger, faster blood to add to their D-line, turning me into an obsolete dinosaur.

Karis cuts her gaze toward me. "We've had a chance to review Ballas's contract and there are a few modifications we'd like to discuss regarding his position with the team..."

I bristle at the level of judgement I hear in her tone and the censorious glaze in her green eyes. Maybe this is how she presents herself during every meeting but it's definitely not the way she looked or sounded when she cried out in sheer pleasure while I was between her legs. But what would I expect?

Considering how I left things—and the way I left her—I suppose I deserve her unfiltered animosity.

Nobody ever said I was a good guy.

But I'm a damn good player. Sure, last year was full of a few ups and downs. Maybe a few more challenges than usual which some people took to mean the beginning of the end, but I finished strong. Which is where I'm at right now. I don't rest on my laurels and hopefully that will keep me in the game for the foreseeable future.

And if anyone in this room besides me knows I don't rest on my laurels, it's Karis. She should remember very well how much stamina I have, considering I went all night long with her. It's that woman—the sexy vixen—I spent the night with.

But it's not the woman here today.

Today's Karis is the buttoned-up, poker-faced franchise owner in a modest gray pantsuit. The silken blonde hair I'd ran my fingers through that night is pulled back into a sleek pony tail that accentuates her straight nose and high cheek-bones. And that prim-as-fuck white blouse gives only the slight hint of those perky tits I'm intimately familiar with.

I remember just how plump they were when I cupped them in my hands. How sweet those pert nipples tasted when I sucked them between my teeth. And exactly how sexy her moans were when my cock slid inside her tight pussy.

That night, we both got a good fucking.

Today it might just be me who gets fucked.

As a restricted free agent, I'm in a precarious situation. With my previous three-year contract expiring, we began negotia-tions late last season but since the Vikings currently hold the rights to my contract, they have the option to either match the contract offer I received from San Francisco Soaring Eagles or trade me in favor of a higher draft pick.

Or they could just hang on to me and drop me back to the third D-pair. Fuck, that would kill my spirit and make me even grumpier than I am normally.

There's a reason I was named the Beast and it's not for my charming charisma and personality. It's my monstrous drive to win and beat our competitors. Unfortunately, that doesn't erase the fact that my ice time was down last year due to some hard hits against the boards and a head injury earlier in the season.

If I were in the team's position—specifically Karis's—I might consider letting me go, too. Something in the way Karis insinuates my play wasn't good enough draws a rash of anger through my bloodstream though.

I lean forward, thunking both elbows on the table.

"What precisely do you need to discuss about my position? In case you weren't aware, Miss Spurlock," I snap, my voice tight with a clear edge to it. I'm suddenly fighting to control a whirl of volatility that's been simmering since she walked into the room. Maybe it's the way Karis sits there seemingly unfazed while holding my career in the palm of her hand. "I played over sixty-five games last season, racking up 950 to my career total. With nineteen minutes a game, I also put up fifty-five assists. I may not be the youngest on the team anymore, but I'm still bringing it every single game. I'm a fucking solid player and if you don't want me, I'll go to San Fran."

Karis lifts a dark-blonde eyebrow, tilting her head to the side, silently assessing me before she finally speaks. "Yes, I'm very aware of your stats, Ballas. I may be new to this team, but I am a professional and certainly not ignorant of my responsibilities as the franchise owner. Contrary to your assumption, I did my homework. I'm very familiar with all your...*data points*. But if you feel the Vikings isn't the right place for you, we can..."

I'm about to lean over to Quincy to tell him I'm done with this ridiculous excuse of a meeting when he chokes out a cough, holding up a hand to halt the shots being fired between Karis and me.

"Whoa, whoa, whoa. There's no reason to jump there right out of the gate. Ballas"—he grasps my shoulder and digs his thumb in deep enough to inflict pain—"simply wants to reiterate his loyalty and commitment to this team. That's all. He's very interested in remaining here this season."

I scoff under my breath and when my eyes flick back to her face, that's when I see it. There's a faint blush that creeps up her neck and into her cheeks.

Hmm...maybe she doesn't hate me after all, maybe she isn't out for revenge, plotting to ruin my career for how I left things with her. Maybe there's another reason for her appearance at this meeting today.

Which begs the question, why? The words fall out of my mouth before I can stop them.

"Why exactly are you here, Karis?"

Quincy inhales sharply and whacks me in the shin with the heel of his shoe. I turn to see a *what the fuck* look in his expression.

When I return my gaze to Karis, her smile is polite, almost patronizing, as she folds her hands on the table in front of her.

She sniffs, her eyes drilling holes in my head. "I may be new to this organization, Ballas, but I'm not unfamiliar with running a billion-dollar sports franchise. Everyone plays their part in making this operation run smoothly. My job is to ensure I'm spending my money in the right places for the *right* assets."

Her shrewd look could knock a man on his ass and takes my breath away. She just scored on the penalty kill, drawing a line in the sand that clearly says, *Don't underestimate my acumen just because I'm young and beautiful.*

Not that I ever would. While I'm surprised by her presence in this meeting, I don't mind it; on the contrary, it shows a lot of balls. It's just not typical for a team owner to join in the contract negotiations of players. Unless there's a concern over salary cap or budget or a high-profile player, the GM normally handles these matters directly and without interference.

If I had to guess, I'd say she doesn't trust Nate to do his job.

Karis taps the screen of the iPad illuminating her face, making her green eyes gleam in the electronic glow. The same green eyes that stared down at me with unbridled lust while I was between her legs and making her orgasm with my tongue.

The memory of how she tasted has me instinctively licking my lips.

Karis raises her head and there's an audible hitch in her breath when she notices my mouth. I know I shouldn't, but I raise my brows as she fumbles with the device, poking the screen with frantic motions.

She clears her throat. "I've asked our analysts to provide me with a summary of the team's strengths and weaknesses based on stats and which position changes they believe will offer us the best lineup next season."

I nod. "Okay. Let's hear it."

Karis offers a tight-lipped smile in return. She turns the device around so Quincy and I can see the colorful and complicated charts and graphs that make no sense to me. I hope they do to her.

"This data, Ballas, indicates that your defensive skills are a strong asset for our organization. You're the defensemen point leader for the Vikings, and aside from that early season concussion last year, you put up some excellent numbers."

Quincy interrupts boastfully on my behalf. "Ballas is ranked in the top five for a defenseman in the entire league, Ms. Spurlock."

Karis glances at Quincy and inclines her head with a polite nod, her ponytail swishing gently from side-to-side. "Yes, precisely. Ballas's physical health aside, it is for this reason we have decided to match the offer you received from the Eagles and extend your contract for another year."

The attorney slides the contract down the table toward Quincy, who begins to review it. I want to slump in relief but instead, straighten against the back of my chair. I never wanted to leave Vancouver. I couldn't see myself playing on any other team than the Vikings.

Many older guys get traded in their final years in order to bring in new blood to the team. The veterans end up having to start over on a new team roster in a different city, with lines they aren't familiar with. I'm too old for that shit, so this is relief to my ears.

Quincy turns the page and gives a low hum of approval, then pushes it in front of me, pointing out the terms with the tip of his finger. I do a quick review and nod.

Karis is about to say something more when Nate interjects his own commentary.

"You'll find the terms and the salary offer more than fair for a player at this point in your career." His tone is condescending and downright rude. Ever since Nate took the position of GM two years ago, he's made my life miserable. There's never been any love lost between us, probably at least in part because I slept with his ex-wife, Alexis, while they were going through their divorce.

The sex was good but maybe not worth the trouble it brought me with Nate in the long run. Or maybe we're just two assholes who don't get along.

I consider the terms of what potentially could be my last NHL contract. It's actually a better offer in the short-term, since my previous contract was for three years totaling $8 million.

My chest unravels like skate laces, loosening the tension that's been there for months.

Beggars can't be choosers. A one-year extension is about as good as it gets for a guy in my position at this point in my career.

I'm just happy to have another year on the ice locked down with no move required. I can remain with the team here in Vancouver, hopefully get us to another Cup run, and see where I go from here. Maybe squeak out another year or two before I hang up my skates with pride.

After that, it's up in the air. I have no plans after retirement and no idea what I want to do. It pains me to think I may have to walk away from the sport that I've loved since I was five years old.

Until that day comes, I just need to keep my focus on the ice.

And not on the ice queen who now owns the organization.

2

———

K aris

I let out a pent-up breath the minute the meeting concludes and exit the room, feeling the sweat that dotted my skin the last thirty minutes drip down my spine and pool at the edge of my waistband.

My God it was hot in that room and so thick with tension that you could slice it with a knife.

Or maybe it was just me trying to keep emotions reined in while speaking to the man I want to despise. Instead, I made a business decision to keep him on my team, which meant wearing my poker face and keeping cool under the weight of seeing him again, a scenario I never thought would happen.

It's not like I'm uncomfortable facing difficult conversations, a very necessary skill in my career. I've done a damn good job of it considering how often I deal with men who think I'm not capable of being at the same table as them. I never let them see me flustered and can keep my composure even during the most challenging situations.

It's likely why I've been labeled an ice queen. I get it. Woman who are tough in business are always labeled and given ridiculously harsh nicknames with the intention of knocking us down a peg.

Do I enjoy being called a name that refers to an icy personality? Absolutely not. Because it's not who I am. I care deeply for people, especially those close to me. But, because of my profession, I use the label and the persona to my advantage to avoid being stepped on.

I'm out of breath from the sprint down to my office, having sped by my administrative assistant, Christine, so fast that I almost miss the funny look she gives me. I normally stop and chit chat, asking her about how her son is doing and how his hockey practice is going. But right now, I need a moment to collect my thoughts and calm down the chaotic whirl in my head that was caused by the only one-night stand I've ever had.

Ballas fucking Keeney.

I could barely breathe in there, suffocated from his presence and the images it conjured up of the two of us together months ago. Had it only been about sex, I could've played it cool with Ballas. We had a night of consensual pleasure with no strings attached. We hooked up and went on our merry way. I was never supposed to run into him again.

But that's not how things ended with Ballas. It involved a hell of a lot more than that, making today's meeting and the decision to keep him on the team a hundred percent more difficult. It's the reason I regarded him with such judgey contempt.

It all came flooding back the moment I saw him again. My intense hatred grew to inferno proportions and threatened to overwhelm me as I went up against a giant asshole who had once offered me comfort and support during my darkest hour, and just as quickly left me dangling alone from the precipice.

I close the door behind me, slumping against it with a thump and berate myself for becoming so agitated in his presence and losing my control.

Don't let him get to you.

Why is it that the one guy I had a one-night fling with happens to be a player on my team?

A knock on my door startles me from my thoughts. I jump upright, gathering the folders and iPad in my hand in a tight grip, and swing around to open it.

Christine stands in the threshold with a cheery smile. She holds out my refillable coffee cup and a new bag of Skittles the size of her head that she must have purchased at Costco and I practically salivate. The two addictions in my life that bring me joy.

"You rushed past me so quick. I didn't get a chance to give these to you." Christine breezes into the office and heads straight toward my desk. She places the coffee on a coaster and then tears open the bag containing my sweet addiction and pours half of it into the crystal candy dish next to my laptop.

Christine tilts her head and eyes me curiously. Her signature silver hoop earrings dangle at her neck and graze the top of her shoulder when she looks back at me.

"Shit, woman. You look...frazzled." She gestures toward my face with a flourish. "And your cheeks are flushed. Are you okay? Does your back hurt? Should I get you an appointment with the team doc?"

Although we haven't worked together all that long, Christine is both intuitive and trustworthy, which is why I've shared with her the details of my car accident and the injuries it left me with.

I wave her off and dip into the dish to retrieve a colorful handful of candy. I pop one in my mouth and sink down into my chair. Sighing, I drop the files on top of a growing pile on my desk.

For the first time today, I relax and let my guard down.

"I'm fine, Christine. No appointment necessary." I take a sip of the strong coffee and clutch the mug in both hands as if it's a lifeline. "I'm just glad that meeting is over and done with."

"Oh? Did it not go as you expected?"

You could say that.

Nothing about Ballas Keeney is what I expected.

I expected him to behave like a grumpy, untamed beast that night in Vegas, which he did. Right up to the point when he turned into a very different version of himself that was more teddy bear than beast.

He shocked and ruined me all in one night.

So, no. Not everything about Ballas is ever what I expect him to be.

I swivel in my chair and stretch out my legs, flopping my head back against the chair headrest with an exasperated sigh.

"Yes and no. I thought I was prepared for him. I thought I was ready to handle it."

My statement has so much more meaning behind it than Christine is aware of. I grappled with my decision to extend his contract through many sleepless nights. I carefully left my personal views out of my verdict. I evaluated his stats through his time in the NHL, especially the numbers he put up with the Vikings the last seven years. The evidence was compelling. But now I wonder if I made a deal with the devil.

I don't necessarily have to see Ballas as the time, but the idea that he's here, right in this building, may be enough to set me over the edge.

It would give Nate pleasure to know just how deeply Ballas gets under my school. My GM was dead set on trading him and in complete opposition of my decision. He wanted Ballas gone and was talking with Coach Thomas on how to rework the lineups.

Unlike my reasons, though, Nate's were all personal. He didn't like Ballas because of his character traits.

"Keeney is cocky and arrogant. He gets himself sent to the bin more times than not. And he's fucking past his prime." Nates vitriol was clear that he hated Ballas nearly as much I do but this is business and we can't risk losing a good player over our personal feelings for him.

Like him or not, Ballas is a beast like no other out on the ice. He can move the puck up the ice and is a great offensive D-man, getting the assists and racking up the points to help the team win.

Sure, Ballas is not a youthful, energetic player. He's grumpy and gets in more scrapes than most and is sent to the penalty box on average more than other players on the team. That part is true. Will Ballas be an unpredictable liability this season? Did I come to the right conclusion?

There's also the teensy-weensy conflict of interest that has now come into play. It hangs over my head like the shoe ready to drop with every choice I'm forced to make.

Based simply on his career, I feel confident that I made the right decision about keeping Ballas on the team. "Always use the numbers," Uncle Marv had said. "They never lie. But gut instinct is also a strong indicator whether a decision is a good one or bad one. That's how the best decisions are made."

Relying on Ballas's stats was a no-brainer. But was it my gut talking when I gave the green light to meet the Eagles' offer sheet? Or something else?

Christine reaches out and is about to remove my coffee cup when I snatch it back, cradling it into my chest as if it's a toy I refuse to share. "Don't. You. Dare. I need this with a desperation you can't even fathom."

This makes her laugh as she stands in front of me expectantly, hands now on her hips.

"I'm not sure anyone can ever really *handle* the Beast," Christine says with a sassy wink. "If you know what I mean. I'm sure that's why you felt off your game. I know I would."

"Christine..." I admonish innocently. "What on Earth are you implying?"

She shrugs, twirling her long tapered fingernail around the big hoop in her ear. "Ballas is a man most people love to hate. Personally, I find those alphahole bad boys irresistible. Case in point, AJ's father, Antoine."

My jaw drops open and I shake my head on a laugh. "At least you ended up with something good out of it with AJ. All I have is a mountain of contracts to review and docs to sign. I'm certain I won't be falling for anyone—bad boy or otherwise—with all the work on my plate."

I unconsciously rub at my lower back which has suddenly awoken and is throbbing with a vengeance. Stress will do that to me.

"Sometimes it just feels like this is too much, you know? I wish Marv were here to help."

Christine gives me a soulful, sympathetic look. "I know, hun. We all miss him and hope for his recovery and return to the helm soon. But you're doing a fantastic job, Karis. Seriously, I don't know how you do it."

Christine has been my uncle Marv's personal assistant for the past four years, ever since he purchased the Vancouver Vikings. She is smart and capable and comes with an undying sense of loyalty and an orneriness that must've been forged while she worked with my uncle before—well, before I took over as owner.

We've had many heart-to-heart discussions over the course of the past six months, usually on the evenings when her ex had her son, when we'd take a moment after the day to share and commiserate over a glass of wine. She knows about my accident. Losing my parents. Living with Uncle Marv. My horrible break-up with Bradley, and now his stalkerish behavior.

Her insight—she seems to have her eyes and ears on everything—has given me a great deal of understanding into the nuances of the organization. I trust her implicitly with nearly everything.

Except for one very intimate detail about Ballas and me.

Christine was the one who called me that night last December to give me the news about my uncle's heart attack. I don't know what I would've done had it not been for her support at the time. She handled all the arrangements to get Marv transported to the ER and was by his side while I was enroute back to Seattle from Vegas that night.

She took care of Marv the same way she now takes care of me. With an unwavering commitment and loyalty.

"Do you want one of those coconut waters you like?" she asks, nodding her chin toward the mini fridge against the far wall. "Those things taste like lukewarm bathwater if you ask me. But you look like you could use some electrolytes or something."

I chuckle and wave her off. "No, I'm okay, really. Why don't you fill me in on my schedule updates for the rest of the week?"

Glancing over her tablet, she spits out a litany of urgent operational requests that have all come through over the last hour.

Maybe she's right and I do need some electrolytes. Or stronger.

"There's been a change in plans too. Nate called a few minutes ago and asked to move up the three o'clock budget meeting to noon." She peers at me through her lashes, brows raised. "That just means he wants a free lunch."

I snort. She doesn't care much for Nate, either.

"The NHL chairman wants to meet with you when he's in town next week. And Petra called. Marek Talbert is asking about some facilities issues with the arena in Seattle."

My temple throbs with the makings of a horrendous headache, which is precisely the reason I need my caffeine and sugar. I drop my head forward into my palms, slowly massaging away the aggravating annoyance that hits me hard out of nowhere.

"Okay." I lift my head, turning back to my open laptop and calendar, as three Slack messages appear in the app box. Christine extracts a boxed water from the fridge, placing it in front of me, and I grudgingly review my schedule changes.

Temporarily running a $1.5 billion NHL franchise, along with my permanent responsibility for a $750 million basketball team, requires careful planning, strategic management, and financial acumen. There's a constant chess game of moving parts, with careers on the line and fans and sponsors to appease.

Which is to say, it's a fucking lot. And if I'm being honest with myself, it's far more than I was ready to take on this early in my career.

At twenty-eight, I'm the youngest owner of an NHL team. Not to mention, only the second female principal owner in the league. It's a lot to manage.

Before my uncle Marv ended up in the hospital, things were substantially easier and under control. At that time, I simply had co-ownership duties for the Puget Sound Pilots basketball organization in Seattle. I also had Marek Talbert, who manages the team with superb leadership skills and taught me about the game of basketball. He has become a great friend to me.

Then my training wheels fell off the night Marv landed in a coma.

My entire world went off-kilter. Marv is the only living family I have left after losing both my parents when I was fifteen and losing him in this manner, along with taking on all this added responsibility is sometimes too much for me to bear alone.

I would never admit feeling overwhelmed to anyone else but Christine. She has my full trust and faith. If it got out to anyone in the NHL about my lack of confidence, it would only give them another reason, besides that I'm a young woman, to criticize or say I'm unqualified to run this organization.

And something tells me that Nate McGowan would just love to use any vulnerability he can find to poke holes in my good name and make himself look better. I don't trust this asshole to have my back like I do with Marek.

In fact, I may need to replace Nate McGowan if things don't turn around with him soon. His contract is also up this year, too, which means I'm in a 'shit or get off the pot' position. I believe Nate must bring something to the table, otherwise my uncle wouldn't have kept him on. The team didn't go to the playoffs last years, so I just haven't figured out yet what it is.

Maybe we'll have a miracle and my uncle will be back to steer the ship before then.

Unfortunately, that's a nearly impossible request because he's lying at home hooked up to machines to keep him alive. It's been months, and I'm at a loss as to what to do.

My heart squeezes at the thought as I finish up with Christine.

"I'm going to run down to the cafeteria to arrange lunch for your budget meeting," she says with a wink, heading toward the door. Then she calls over her shoulder, "And when I return, I'm scheduling you a massage with Kip for later today."

I grumble about to argue with her. "I don't need—"

She cuts me off. "You do and you will. I'll be back."

When the door closes with a click, I open my Inbox and wince. Even though Christine has gone through and prioritized and deleted, I still have over a hundred emails to review and respond to. I'm going to need more coffee for this.

Speaking of which, I think Christine is back when there's another knock on my door.

I don't bother to look up.

"Back so soon?"

The sound of a deep, masculine voice rumbles through the office. Tearing my gaze from my email, I lift my head and stare up at the six-foot-five hockey player standing at the threshold.

One look at Ballas makes my cheeks flame hot and my body flicker alive. Damn him for being so insanely attractive in his tailored navy suit that tugs around his sculpted shoulders and thighs.

Don't let him in. Both figuratively and literally.

"Karis, we need to talk."

He doesn't even bother to ask me if I have time, he just shuts the door behind him and strides forward like he owns the place. Like he owns me.

Well, joke's on him. I own *his* ass.

I do my best to reengage my ice queen mask to appear calm, when on the inside, I'm anything but that. My body lights up like the red lamp when a goal hits the back of the net, but it's not from desire. This time, it's with annoyance over the interruption and resentment over him just barging in like this.

Pull yourself together, Karis. He's not worth your tears or time. He's just another player—in all definitions of the word.

A player who used me, then held me in his arms while I cried, then walked away and forgot about me.

I wish I could scrub my memory and focus only on Ballas's dickish behavior. But I can't because I also know there's a decent man underneath the grouchy exterior. He blew away my preconceived notions last Christmas Eve, the night my uncle was admitted to the hospital.

Ballas showed up unexpectedly in Seattle and was there by my side the entire night. The man who held my hand and let me cry on his shoulder, knowing I had no one else in the world I could lean on.

It's *that* Ballas I want to forget.

I need to remember him the man who shattered my faith when he left without a word of goodbye—no message or note, no follow-up text or call. Ballas Keeney ghosted me, disappearing without a trace, until the moment he sat across the table this morning.

If I allowed my pride to rule my decisions, I would have. But this team means everything to my uncle, and business always comes first. I refuse to make choices that will impact the team based on my heart, feelings or emotional state.

I can, however, boot him out of my office because I'm his motherfucking boss.

"Ballas, there is nothing more we need to discuss. You have your contract and another year on the team. Now, please leave."

But I can't help the words that escape my mouth when I mutter, *"You're good at that."*

3

———

B allas

I realize any conversation that begins with, "We need to talk" is going to border on being unpleasant and potentially unwanted on one of the participants' behalf.

In this case, I'd say it went over like a puck to the chin.

The cold-shoulder treatment is right in line with how I saw this going. I don't begrudge Karis for being pissed off at me for barging in uninvited, either. I'd be considered delusional if I had ever expected her to welcome me with open arms and a cheery smile after my douchebag disappearing act last December.

I'd hoped she could at least hear me out and allow me to apologize. I came up to clear the air about my actions last Christmas. My behavior was reprehensible by most standards, even though pretty typical of me.

An apology is long overdue and also the only way I can see to start fresh and avoid any awkward future interactions between us now that my position is solid on the team. Karis just needs to hear me out.

I stride further into her office. With each step, I practice the words I've rehearsed in my head.

"I'm sorry, I was an asshole. I shouldn't have left you without an explanation. I should have been a friend when you needed one."

Karis glowers at me so strongly I feel the need to look away to avoid the scrutiny in her glare. But I stay the course, as she grows noticeably less composed and more fidgety the closer I get to her desk. Her creamy skin, pale and untouched by the sun, brightens to a deep pink hue. She flicks a lock of hair out of her face and she straightens her spine like she's preparing for battle.

I raise my arms in the air in the sign of surrender.

"Karis, please. Five minutes, that's all I ask."

Karis peers up and past my shoulder toward the window of her office. I follow her gaze, turning my head until Christine's empty desk comes into view.

"Christine's gone. I ran into her at the elevator. If you're worried about privacy..."

She shakes her head vehemently, wisps of blonde hair escaping from her ponytail and falling into her face. Karis tucks some of the loose strands behind her ears and pushes to her feet.

"I'm not worried because we don't need privacy." Her voice is tense and her eyes meet mine as she rounds the side of the desk before coming to an abrupt stop at the corner. She casts a downward glance her fitness watch and then bristles.

"I'm busy, Ballas, and don't have five minutes. There is nothing we have to discuss, and I'm late for my next meeting."

She picks up the phone and iPad from her desk, bending so her white blouse stretches and clings to the curve of her waist. I take another step forward, and catch a whiff of her soft, feminine scent. The same fragrance that has lingered in my memories since the night we were together.

Covering her hand gently with my palm, I press it down to the desk.

"No, you're not."

Karis stammers in a bewildered and guarded tone, snatching her wrist away.

"Are you also my new admin and know everything about my schedule, Ballas?"

I chuckle and drop my hand to my side while the corners of my mouth tip into an amused grin. "I asked Christine if you were available."

She *pffts*, and swivels quickly, leaving her devices on the desk in favor of crossing her arms with a cute growl of irritability. "Remind me to fire her."

I laugh at her fake outrage as she sits back down with a sneer, her mouth twisting in a grimace of indignation.

This fiery woman is the same one who boldly stated she wanted me to fuck her that night in Vegas and then quickly showed me her vulnerabilities and inexperience. The two sides of Karis Spurlock are the reasons I haven't been able to get her out of my head since then.

She slips a manicured finger into a brightly colored candy dish, fishing around to pluck out a few red Skittles before parting her lips and popping them in her mouth. I stare with fascination at those perfect lips as they open and close around the candy. The tip of her pink tongue peeks out, sending a flood of memory back to my brain.

And my cock.

Which is precisely why I need to steer clear of those memories, make amends, and find a way to co-exist in this new team environment. Forge ahead past my mistake and start over on a professional level.

And what a fucking mistake it was. It serves me right for trying to be the kind of man she needed when I obviously couldn't pull it off.

That night I did something completely out of character for me. I stepped out on a limb and I offered my support and shoulder for Karis to cry on when her uncle landed in the hospital.

As they say, no good deed goes unpunished.

It took me four hours to realize she needed something far more than I was able to offer. I'm just not a man equipped with the level of emotional resonance required in that situation.

Sex? I can give that.

A hug of encouragement? That's easy enough.

But to stick it out and stay by a woman's side during her time of need?

Not in my wheelhouse.

So, I did the only thing I could do. I ran.

Now I'm stuck with the repercussions of that decision and I'm now on the receiving end of Karis's icy glare.

"Karis, will you let me explain?"

Her green eyes grow cold and dark with contempt. She pushes out of her chair again, sending it careening wildly back into the bookshelf behind her. Several trophies and plaques displayed on the shelves wobble precariously. She moves over to the bank of windows looking out over the cityscape, standing stiffly as she shifts indignantly from foot to foot.

"The clock started ticking two minutes ago. You've got three minutes left. Hurry up and get on with it so you can leave." She hooks a thumb toward the door but her voice quivers slightly enough for me to tell the fire is weakening in her resolve.

There's a flash of something in her bright eyes as they narrow at me before she turns away again. I almost forgot how stunningly beautiful she is, and strong. The kind of beauty that knocks men off their feet and the type of strength that puts even hockey players like me to shame.

I'm not called Ballas the Beast because I'm sweet and cuddly. I'm a six-foot-five Oscar the Grouch on a pair of motherfucking skates.

But one night with Karis turned me into a gooey sap, and it scared me shitless.

When she had looked up at me while we sat vigil for her uncle, tears glistening in her eyes, with such need for stability, like I was some kind of savior or knight in shining armor,

I panicked. I am no one's goddamn savior. I don't have an empathetic bone in my body and she was pinning her hopes on me to be there when she needed someone the most?

Not a chance in hell was I that guy and I didn't want to give her that impression, which would've happened had I stayed. The moment she'd fallen asleep, slumped in in the uncomfortable hospital chair next to Marv's bed, I took off and hightailed it back to Vancouver. I didn't look back. No goodbye, no number given, no thoughtful floral arrangement and sweet condolence card left on a piece of paper on the night table by her uncle's bed.

I was a chickenshit and ran as fast as I could in the other direction.

Jesus, now that I think about it, maybe my rehearsed apology speech won't even come close to mending the hole I dug for myself.

I never expected we'd be in the same room together again. She lives in Seattle and oversees the ownership responsibilities for a basketball team. I'm in Vancouver and play hockey.

Then everything changed in a strange and tragic twist of fate when Marv Spurlock slipped into a coma and she was the beneficiary of all his businesses.

Which leaves me here to clean up the mess I made with the woman who stubbornly refuses to look at me or allow me to apologize.

I take a tentative step toward her, so close now that I can smell the sweet candy on her breath.

"You have every right to be furious with me. I deserve it."

She whips back around and her shoulder brushes against my chest. A patronizing smile lift at the corners of her mouth, her tone bone-dry. "Why would I be mad? You—" she gestures between us—"mean nothing more to me than a name on my team roster. You, Ballas Keeney, are just a hockey player."

Damn. That one was a solid puck shot to the gut.

A steely expression curtains over her face, betraying nothing but polite professionalism now. She takes a step back and shoves a delicate hand out at me to shake.

I should just shake her hand and be on my way. Let this serve as a lesson to me for any future interactions I have with Karis Spurlock. She despises me and there's no apology I can give that will change that.

There's a hundred and one reasons why I should just turn around and walk out that door and leave this conversation behind. And why I shouldn't do something as stupid as kissing her.

First and foremost being our working relationship.

Karis is not simply some random hookup anymore. She's the team owner and my boss's new boss.

Second, kissing her now would be imprudent, not to mention highly inappropriate.

And third, she obviously hates me.

Karis hates me with the same level of intensity as the Boston Bruins hate the Montreal Canadiens.

Or at the very least, she strongly dislikes this situation we've gotten ourselves into. Therefore, there is no doubt she wouldn't want me to touch her, much less kiss her.

Yet none of that stops me from what I do next.

Taking a solid step into her space, I snag her wrist, tug her into my chest, and throw caution to the wind when I crush my mouth to hers.

Her next words die on her tongue, her breath hitches, and I swallow down her gasp of angry surprise. Karis pushes at my chest with her palm. I pause to peer down at her, hoping to read her expression. Her mouth opens and she lets out a shuttering breath.

I pull back, ready to walk away and in an instant, Karis grabs onto the back of my head and crushes her mouth against mine.

Something inside of me snaps and I waste no time, my tongue raiding in a claiming stroke. I do a mental fist pump and victory lap.

I wrap an arm around her lower back and splay my fingers wide, holding her solidly against me. Her fingers spear through my hair and with a savage ferocity.

The kiss is urgent and fiery. Punishing and hostile.

I'm searching for forgiveness. She's looking for revenge.

Karis pushes on her tiptoes and tugs the strands clasped in her tight grasp. The cruel ravishment and exploration between us is a heady cocktail, quick to ignite my body with needy lust.

I want to serve out my penance between her legs. This

woman could make me beg if she wanted to. Beg for forgiveness that I would give her in spades.

But that's not what's going to happen.

The knock on the door followed by the sound of her name being called as it opens douses the flames of passion before we can even register the burn. Karis jerks out of my hold and severs our kiss.

With a muffled curse, she flings herself away from my body, only stopping when she grabs onto the back of the visitor's chair.

I run a hand over my stubbled jawline, then reach for her elbow. She takes another step away, putting more space between us. Her eyes bore into mine, as if deploring me to keep my distance and keep quiet, before she breaks that connection and shakes her head.

Clearing her throat, she smooths a hand over her stomach, gathering her composure once again reverting back to boss lady.

"Thank you, Ballas. I appreciate you stopping by to check on my uncle. I'll be sure to tell him you said hello."

I quirk an eyebrow at her ease in recovery. She's quick on her feet, I'll give her that. I'm still lost in the moment, my scalp throbbing where her fingers yanked at my hair.

And that's not the only thing left throbbing.

I drop my hands in front of my tented pants and ignore the painful ache in my balls as the door opens wider as a young woman pops her head into the office.

"Come on in," she calls out while I start counting to a hundred in order to calm my body down.

"I'm sorry to interrupt, Ms. Spurlock," the young woman stammers as she glances between Karis and me with nervous regret. Her cheeks blush to match the oversized pink glasses perched on her nose. "Oh! Hello, Ballas. I didn't mean to...I just saw Christine and she said I could stop by with the new samples we received for this upcoming season's team gear."

Karis nods and returns to her desk, waving the young woman in as she takes a seat.

"Of course, Amie. Come on over and show me what you've got. Ballas was just on his way out." With one raised eyebrow, she gives me a dismissive glance. "We'll see you when the season resumes, Ballas. Have a nice summer."

I dip my chin, nodding to both women as I exit the office, pulling the door closed behind me.

I'm not sure if my aborted apology made any sort of progress on smoothing things out between Karis and me or if that kiss only added to a growing list of reasons for her to despise me. Whatever the case, all I know is that kiss will be in constant rotation in my dreams every night this summer.

Who needs rest in the offseason anyway?

4

———

Karis – August

The summer passed by in a blur of meetings, travel, and the constant checking in after Uncle Marv's care. I was down in several times a month for said meetings with the Pilots' team management and would stop by for updates from his private care team.

To say it's been a difficult task is an understatement.

Add to that all the business and work I had on my plate, I barely had time to eat sensibly and manage some self-care. There was no personal time outside of that, which meant no time for dating, either. And no time to contemplate that kiss Ballas left me in my office the day of his contract extension meeting.

Yet somehow, regardless of my best intentions, he managed to infiltrate my dreams every night this summer. I'd fall asleep then wake from a fitful sleep, sweaty and horny, wrapped up in a haze of sexy fantasies with the need for that other '*self*' care time. Arguably, dreaming of Ballas between my legs was never quite as satisfying as the real thing.

Just to make matters worse, my ex-boyfriend, Bradley, the man I dumped back in December because he cheated on me, has decided, after months of playing the field, that he wants to get back together. He's been calling nearly every day—even though I've yet to answer the phone—and sends me texts, emails, floral arrangements, and baskets of my favorite goodies.

Today features yet another overpriced, unwanted delivery. I scowl at the arrangement that just arrived and have a burning urge to throw them against the wall.

That would be satisfying except then I'd just have to clean up the mess left behind.

Normally, I'd ask Christine to dispose of them, but she's on a well-deserved vacation this week before all the players and admins return for the start of pre-season practice and training camp.

A strange thread of awareness prickles down my spine when I think of seeing Ballas again. I pick up the glass vase, indulging in the succulent scent of the beautiful, but unwanted flowers, and carry it with me to the elevator.

I shouldn't have read the note attached but I caved. His words were not only cringe-worthy but so revealing of Bradley's narcissism.

"Sunshine,

Please call me back. I know I made a mistake when I let you go. I still love you. You're the one for me.

Love, Bradley."

The fact that he believes he let me go has me snorting out loud as I press the button on the elevator door to head down to the parking garage to throw out the reminder of him. Bradley's indiscretions and his inability to keep his dick in his pants during our time together became the deciding factor for my decision to break it off with him.

A woman deserves a man who builds her up and worships her, not a douche who puts her down.

It was on my way to Vegas when I finally came to that realization and became a new woman. It all led me to my one-night fling with Ballas.

The flowers are just another reminder of how happy I am to be single again and not with that dog. He's delusional if he thinks he can win me back by sending a few over-priced and extravagant gifts.

I don't have time for his bullshit—which borders now on stalkerish behavior. But at least I now realize my worth and know I am deserving of more than he could ever give me.

I give my head a shake and shove my nose into the lilies, taking in one last sniff of the fragrance of my favorite flowers. Once I ditch these in the garbage dumpster, I'll go grab some lunch from the vending machine.

When the buzzer dings and the doors open, I take a step forward off the elevator, my nose still buried in the arrangement and I run smack dab into a wall of human.

"Oomph." The air is knocked out of my lungs and I'm thrown off-kilter. I back up to regain my balance, embarrassed that I hadn't been paying attention to where I'm going. "I'm so sorry. Excuse me…"

A large pair of hands grab the heavy glass vase from my grasp, shifting it to the side and away from my face.

Ballas.

Speak of the devil.

He oh-so-casually tips his chin in a nod, his eyes bouncing from the flowers to my eyes, a slow smile inching up at the corners of his mouth. He drops his warm hands from the vase. I take a step back from the open elevator door.

Regaining my composure, I steel my resolve and stifle the part of me that is thrilled to see him again, working to maintain a professional aloofness.

"Good to see you, Ms. Spurlock." His low timber voice shakes me to my very core, already unraveling any hope I had to remain cool and unaffected. Dammit, I want to stay mad at him.

Placing his back against the door to keep it from closing, he crosses one ankle over the other and casually leans back. "Celebrating something, or is someone in the doghouse?"

It's annoying how gorgeous he looks. His handsome face sports a golden tan that's probably the outcome of months out on a fishing boat or golf course. Christine, who is always good for all the juicy comings-and-goings of the organization, mentioned something about his whereabouts this summer and had numerous stories to share about what she heard of his well-known conquests and revolving door of lovers.

Fighting the pang of jealousy that poked at my heart's edges, I resisted the urge to inquire more about it and clamped my mouth shut like the proud woman I am, gently reminding myself that I didn't give a rat's ass about Ballas, his trip, or his current relationship status.

Lies. All lies.

Honestly, it proved more difficult than I had hoped this past summer to remember why Ballas should mean nothing to me. It's as if the kiss we shared in my office that day worked some magic spell, charming me out of all the animosity I'd had toward him.

His voice is full of amusement but is that interest in his eyes? Is he asking if I'm seeing someone?

I carefully hide my own flicker of interest with forced composure, trying hard not to breathe in his spicy, woodsy scent that makes my brain go a little fuzzy. What'd he ask me again?

"It's none of your business, Ballas." I scoff with a roll of my eyes. "But if you must know, I'm throwing these away because that doghouse was burned to the ground and the dog was sent off when he humped another bitch."

He chokes out a loud rumbling laugh and somehow the movement of his body causes the elevator to shake so that the too-heavy vase wobbles in my other arms.

Ballas swiftly swings and arm out and he settles a large hand on the bottom of the vase to prevent it from falling.

"Whoa, there, sweetheart," he says in a smooth tone that's rich with an intimacy reserved for lovers.

The reminder that we were lovers makes me want to throat punch him—or kiss that sexy mouth of his.

The next thing I know, he's standing right in front of me, tall and broad-shouldered and taking over my entire field of vision. His breath smells like a minty gum and reminds me of how he tasted the last time I saw him. His cologne is rich and spicy like cinnamon and orange. It's a warm scent, not overpowering and artificial like that of so many men I come across in this business, that scent loved by power-hungry men who try to impress women with money and prestige.

Like Bradley.

The doors suddenly close behind him with a *whoosh* and my heart leaps into my throat from being so close in this isolated, cramped space.

"Here, let me help you. It's awfully heavy."

I twist away in haughty obstinance. "I'm fine. I can handle it."

"Fine." He backs away with his hands up. As he turns, he murmurs under his breath, "I remember you can handle big things in your grip."

I make a sound of indignation at the clearly suggestive comment. It was sexual, wasn't it? Or am I just reading into it?

"Watch yourself, Ballas," I warn, heat flaming across my cheeks even as my panties dampen. I don't know if I should be turned on by his dirty talk or annoyed that he's using our past intimacy against me. "Watch your mouth. You forget who I am and where we're at."

"Oh, I know exactly who you are, Karis," he says smugly, his eyes brimming with challenge as they rake over me. I hold my ground, willing myself not to cave under the intensity of his gaze. He points a finger toward me and twirls it. "Underneath all this, I know what you want, too."

There's a challenge and a demand in them that has me torn between wanting him to take me like he owns me and pushing him away for fear I'll lose myself in him.

His gaze moves to my lips and lingers. "As for my mouth, you didn't mind it so much when I told you to spread your legs and made you come with my mouth on your pussy."

I let out a nearly hysterical huff and try to skirt around him, to get off the elevator so I can get some air. My head is starting to fog. There's a restless energy that vibrates through his movement, a power that coils within him that's devastatingly appealing and is leaving me in a sexual haze. His tantalizing scent, and powerful set of his shoulders give him an air of command that exudes from every pore.

He makes me weak. And that makes me mad.

"Out. Of. My. Way."

I finally shove past him but years of shutting down the best goal-scorers in the world makes him agile, and he quickly moves in front of me just inside the parking garage and spins me around. He cages me against the cement block wall and then leans down.

For a moment, I think he's going to take the vase and bend down to kiss me. My heart beats wildly against my ribs, taking my breath as I wait for his mouth to firmly press against mine.

Instead, he grabs the card hidden between the stems and extracts it from the envelope.

"Hey! That's personal." My obvious irritation over not getting kissed comes out in a bratty whine. Any attempt to rescue the card from his fingers is utterly futile since he's a good six inches taller than me and I'm still holding the vase tightly against my body.

I growl like a baby tiger against an untamed lion.

He narrows his eyes on the card.

"Sunshine, Please call me back. I know I made a mistake when I let you go. I still love you. You're the one for me. Love, Bradley."

Although I know what it says since I've already read it, it sounds even more ridiculous read out loud in a high falsetto voice he uses. I stifle my laugh by biting down on my lower lip.

Ballas glances down and raises one eyebrow in disbelief, then fans the card in the air. "*Whoowee*," he whistles and expels in an exaggerated drawl. "What a fucking dipshit. That's the worst apology I've ever read."

My cheeks burn with embarrassment, although I don't know why. I didn't ask Bradley to send me flowers or his lame-ass apology.

"You mean, besides the one you tried to give me?" I put on my best saccharine-sweet smile.

He laughs wryly. "To be fair, when I rehearsed it in my head it sounded great. It just had trouble making it out of here." He taps on the card on his lips before shoving it back into the bouquet. "At least now I understand why you're ditching these."

I raise a skeptical eyebrow. "And what do you know about him?"

Ballas looks like he's about to say something but shakes his head instead. "Nothing, I guess."

"When was the last time you ever sent an apology bouquet to a woman?"

He merely shrugs a shoulder and mumbles, "Never sent a bouquet to anyone before period. You're the first woman I ever had to apol..." His words linger in the air between us, much like the overwhelming fragrance of the floral arrangement. "Forget it."

His statement floors me and I want badly to follow it up with additional questions about his past dating history and personal life. Instead, I remember what I came down here for, and it wasn't to be grilled by Ballas or to interrogate him.

"That's what I thought," I answer shortly. "For someone who by his own admission doesn't do relationships or feel the need to send a woman flowers, you sure have a lot to say about the whole process."

With a smack of his palm, he places his hand above my head and with a deliberately casual move, whisks the vase from my grip in the other hand. Then he leans forward, his mouth hovering within inches of mine. I swallow hard.

In a controlled voice, he says, "Maybe I'm just curious about your love life, Miss Spurlock."

He winks and pulls away, gesturing with a wide sweep of his arm out into the parking lot toward the dumpsters in the back. I brush past him, empty handed, as he follows me toward the bins.

"I don't need your input on my love life, Ballas." I grouse over my shoulder at him. I want to add, *you gave up that privilege months ago,* but I bite my tongue and take the high road —something he clearly can't do.

When I get to the large commercial dumpster, I swing around in front of him and grab for the vase, jockeying for the stupid flowers that are just going to be thrown away in the trash. Ballas has gotten my emotions all stirred up. Why does he fluster me so much? Why can't I just act normal around him instead of feeling this mix of sexual heat and frustration?

When I clasp my fingers around the vase, they graze over his knuckles, and the heat of his skin radiates through my hand and up my arm. My breath catches and I tamp down that zap of chemical reaction, staring him down with a steely gaze. "All I need from you, Ballas, is for you to help the team win games this season. That's it."

Ballas shrugs and then lifts the container lid, motioning with his chin toward it.

"Let 'er rip, Karis," he encourages with a wink. "And remind me never to buy you flowers."

I throw the vase and its entire contents into the bin and fight down a grin when I hear it shatter into pieces with a satisfying crash.

Wiping my hands, I spin on my heels and head toward the building entrance.

"Contrary to popular belief," I say over my shoulder as he watches me walk away from him, "A woman doesn't need a man to buy her flowers. She just needs him to treat her right."

And stick around when we need you.

5

———

Ballas

"That's it, man. Ten more. You got this, B."

Roland, the team's head trainer, counts out reps for me, encouraging me along as he's done countless times before and pushing me when I fall behind.

Which seems to be happening more and more these days, especially this morning because my mind isn't in this weight room with me.

It's stuck on that conversation with Karis earlier in the parking garage and the way I behaved toward her. I acted like a complete and utter asshole.

I have two theories on why that is, which I happened to ruminate on over the entire summer.

The first is that I can't come to terms with my age and where I'm at in my career. It seems like just yesterday that I was a twenty-four-year-old elite d-man, being touted as the best in the league, strutting around like a cocky player.

And look at me now? Sweat dripping into my eyes and mouth, heaving for breath with the salty taste sticking on my tongue like a bad omen.

I stop after eight reps, wheezing like a longtime smoker, as I conjure up the image of Karis as she walked away from me earlier.

That was as painful for me as this last set of dead lifts. Truth be told, she consumed my thoughts all goddamn summer, no matter where I was, what I was doing, or who I was doing them with. It pissed me off that I couldn't get her out of my head. Which is probably why I was such a dick to her this morning.

I'm just racking up the tally for apologies owed, aren't I?

Roland scoffs loudly, giving me a nudge of my hip. "Come on, bro. You want me to start calling you old man?"

I give him a sneering glare and flip him off around the iron bar bell that's still in my grip.

"Not one more fucking word," I rasp, using the most intimidating voice I can. He only laughs.

Roland Terry has been the team's strength and conditioning coach since before I joined the team. He's a great guy who has seen me through many of my minor injuries, including the hit I sustained last season and the resulting concussion.

Ro cocks a brow and then mimes zipping his mouth shut with a quirk of his lips.

We finish out the reps and I take a break, grabbing my water bottle and towel hanging on the bar next to me and swiping at the sweat pouring down my neck. I bend at the waist, throwing the towel over my head, and prop my elbows on my thighs, panting loudly with exhaustion.

"When did your workouts get so hard?" I grumble, taking another swig of my water and giving Ro a sideways glance. "Fucking hell. Maybe I didn't keep up on my conditioning this summer the way I thought I did."

"You're only as old as you feel." Ro pats me on the back and chuckles kindly. "We'll get you back to the Beast in no time."

Thank God I still have time. I took it upon myself to get back into the weight room early, even though the official pre-season training isn't scheduled to begin until next week.

Even though I still did some training for the last two months, I took a much-needed break from my usual routines to allow my body to rest. It had taken a beating when I dove back into playing hockey after Christmas.

With my head a mess over what had happened between Karis and me, I returned to the ice and gave more than a hundred and ten percent in every game for the remainder of the season. I took out all my frustration and confusion against our opponents, especially when we were up against the team of my long-time adversary, Sergei Russo.

I'd spent my summer being active, but relaxing, out on the open water and on the links. The distance and time helped me forget about the strange, unwanted feelings I had for Karis.

I was a fucking idiot for getting carried away and kissing her.

Never in all my history of hookups and one-nighters have I

gone back for seconds or pursued anything more meaningful with a woman. So why did I kiss her again?

I decided to chalk it up to getting older and more sentimental as I inch toward my hockey retirement. With my career nearing its end, the fear of the unknown continues to mount with uncertainty for what my future holds. I guess you could say I'm burying my head in the sand trying to avoid making plans. My sole focus is on this coming season.

If this is going to be my final season, I want to go out with a bang. So I decided to come back from my vacation early and check in on how the rookie training camp is going. I plan to swing by tomorrow to see all the new recruits in action, especially the young kid, Shaw Benning.

Speaking of young kid, a voice from the doorway has me glancing over my shoulder to see my teammate, Cale Costa, strutting in with that cocky swagger of his.

"I heard a lot of whining and bitching coming from in here. Thought I'd check things out in case old man, Keeners, fell down and couldn't get back up. Where is your walker, by the way? "

Cale throws his bag on a bench with an uproariously loud laugh and stops in front of me. He knocks his knuckles against my shoulder and then throws a hand out for a one-handed fist bump. I glare up at last year's team captain and frown.

"Fuck you, Costa." I shove him good-naturedly in his ribs and he sidesteps with a laugh. "Maybe you should put your money where your mouth is. Let's see if you still got it, eh, Costa?"

He sits on the workout bench across from us and gives a "Hey, Ro," before turning back to me.

"Jesus, Keeners. You must be really worried about that old body of yours if you're here this early," he teases, shaking his head in displeasure. "That might not bode well for us winning the Cup this season."

I snort. "Dude, you're in pretty early yourself. What's up with that? You still working on that knee?"

Cale is one of the best two-way wingers in the league. He's proven his worth during his first three years with the Vikings, only to get in a nasty collision on the ice last season. He absorbed a low hit along the boards, which resulted in a season-ending injury to his knee.

I called to check in on him a few times throughout the summer. He was disappointed, as any one of us would be, to spend his summer rehabbing. But when we talked in June after my contract renewal, he promised he was back in business and was committed to getting back so he could play all 82 games this coming year.

Cale smacks his leg with his hand and cups a palm around his left knee to lift it up.

"Nah, brah. It's all good. Spent the last few months getting healthy and ready to go with the help of some great professionals back in Ontario."

I raise my brow. "And maybe some help of the female persuasion, too?"

He snickers and shrugs it off. "That's a given. Puck bunnies are always in season. How about you, Keeners? Is your grumpy ass still chasing 'em?"

"As long as I can, bro. Not looking to settle down anytime soon," I quip back. "Staying single sure makes life a hell of a lot easier when it's just your own bag to pack if you're traded."

"I guess." Cale nods in agreement. "Getting kind of tired of the single life though. Only so much clubbing you can do until it becomes boring as fuck."

"Dude, then you're doing it wrong," says a voice from the other side of the weight room. We both look over to see one of our forwards, Dane Axelrod, geared up in sweats and a T-shirt and pushing through the locker room doors.

He walks over and claps us both on our backs, smiling broadly to show off where a tooth used to be missing. Looks like he had some dental work this summer because he now has a complete set of pearly whites.

"Hey, Ax. Good to see you, brah," Cale says, clasping his hand in greeting. They do their usual convoluted handshake that ends with both of them bent over at the waist and clapping each other's hands like a climbing ladder until their hands are on the other guy's head and they ruffle their hair. I shake my own head and grumble at their ridiculousness. Maybe someday they'll grow up.

"How was your summer, boys?" Ax asks, stepping up onto one of the treadmills to begin an easy jog.

"Mine was okay. It'd have been better without this." He pats his knee and Ax nods in sympathy. I'd have rather had Keener's summer plans though. Didn't you go fishing somewhere in Bali?" Cale asks me.

"Baja, then Fiji. Did some golfing, too."

"Whoa, epic, dude," exclaims Ax, his expression reminding me just how young he still is. He was drafted at nineteen and he's only twenty-one or two now. "Bet you caught a lot more than fish down there, eh?"

"Just hope it wasn't a STI," Cale teases with a wink as he leans over and smacks my bare leg.

Axelrod laughs. "Yeah, man. Good thing we get tested before the season starts so they can put you on some antibiotics, Keeners."

I ignore their stupid commentary about my sexual health because I know I have nothing to prove and nothing to worry about.

Yes, I had all summer to sleep around with bikini-clad single women, but did I?

No, because none of them were Karis.

Something about Karis Spurlock has fucked me up in the head and messed with my mojo.

And I don't know what to do about it.

6

___

K aris

"I think you'll be happy with the trade we just acquired," I say in an over-bright voice while running a brush through my uncle's stark white hair.

It had been a salt-and-pepper gray until he fell into this coma, brought on by the anoxic brain injury when he was in surgery and deprived of oxygen. It may be snowy white now, but it's still the same thick head of hair he was always so proud of.

I set the brush down on the bedside table and adjust Marv's covers. We moved him from a rehab facility in Seattle back to his home in late April, right after the Vikings lost in the first round of the finals. Moving him after the team lost gave me the opportunity to spend the time needed to find suitable round-the-clock in-home care. Although not easy to find, the task is made a lot less difficult when money is no object.

In fact, I'd been referred to the company by the Viking's head trainer, so I knew it was a reputable business. The owner and ARNP, Daria Rupp, is a godsend and has made the considerable number of decisions I've had to make less draining on me emotionally with the caring guidance she provides.

I bend over and place a kiss on Marv's forehead. Having been confined to a bed for months—hooked up on a dialysis machine, ventilation, and feeding tubes—he has aged so much and looks much older than his sixty-two years. I gently stroke his hair and talk to him as if nothing were amiss and we're just having a normal everyday conversation.

While it's rare for someone to remain in this type of coma for so long, I made the decision that I thought was best and am giving Marv the care I know he deserves. I consulted with numerous doctors and specialists along the way and came to the conclusion they all differed on the opinion whether or not Marv can hear me or even comprehend what I'm saying.

But I still continue to hold my one-sided conversations because it helps me to talk through the team changes. By sharing the details and keeping him informed, I feel less alone and not like I'm shouldering the burden of two teams on my own.

I hold out hope that Marv will pull through soon. He'll wake up, breeze through rehab as if nothing ever happened and resume his ownership responsibilities, relieving me of my temporary duties.

It's what I have to believe in order to get through this tragedy without curling up in a ball and drowning myself in tears of grief. Marv's the only one I have left in this world and I can't bear the thought of him gone, leaving me a complete orphan. No parents. No family. Just me.

I continue to elaborate on the recent team changes for the Vikings that Nate and our new head coach, Conner Thomas, worked out with me. "We were able to lock down Nils Lundren from the Nighthawks with a one-year contract. If you remember, he became a free agent at the end of last season. Nate mentioned you were eager to get him signed when he became eligible."

Nate, Conner, and I met early last week, right before training camp began, and ran through our roster, all subject to change when we cut the list in half after training camp. Conner—a thirty-year veteran of hockey and the father of current NHL superstar Callan Thomas—had some great insight right out of the shoot on how the team could capitalize off the already strong defensive line and who he thought would work best with current players.

Conner thought we could experiment with Nils, Ballas, and last year's captain, Cale. Nate hated the idea.

However, with a new coach on board and Nate's cantankerous attitude, I thought it best that I be around to at least offer some thoughts and provide a third opinion if there were any head-to-head disputes.

Getting to know Conner has eased my mind about the team and chances winning the Cup on our upcoming season. Coach Thomas is an affable man. Nate, however, continues to give off a strange vibe, like he's a villain in a Shakespeare play and every time I see him staring at me, as if I'm on his list to kill off.

Nate aside, I'm grateful to have other strong staff members on both the Vikings and my Pilots teams to rely on because otherwise I might just collapse under the heavy weight of stress.

I never thought I'd be at this juncture in my life. Having been orphaned at fifteen when my parents died in the car accident that also gave me a life-threatening injury, I thought my resilience was pretty sound, that I was more than strong enough to handle all my uncle's business expected of me during his incapacity.

But this has been a level of trauma and pressure I've never known before.

As Marv's sole heir, beneficiary, successor trustee, and the executor of his will, I've been tasked with temporarily running the entirety of his empire, including his two professional sports clubs located in different cities and several other, smaller businesses, which thankfully have people running the daily operations.

It would be a daunting and overwhelming task for anyone, but especially someone who barely has two years of real-world experience under her belt.

Somehow, I manage to get through the long days of endless meetings and executive decisions, only to crawl into bed exhausted with a bone-deep loneliness, sobbing until I have no more tears to cry. The weight of missing my uncle, even though he's physically still here, is soul crushing. Apart from Daria, who has become as much of a friend to me as she is a caregiver to Marv, there's nobody for me to lean on for support either.

At that thought, my chest tightens to the point where I can barely breathe.

"I was hoping to see you this week."

I lift my head from where I'd laid it down next to Marv to see Daria as she enters my uncle's room. A stethoscope is looped around her elegant neck, and her dark pixie curls are pinned back from her forehead with an ornate barrette. She strides gracefully toward me as I stand and enclose my arms around her.

"It's so good to see you," I murmur over her shoulder, tears prickling behind my eyes. My five-foot-six frame casts a shadow over her tiny five-foot-nothing body. But for what she lacks in height, she brings with heart. I don't know what I would have done without her gentle spirit and angelic fierceness.

She pulls back and peers up at me with her intuitive gaze.

"What's going on with you? You don't look like you're getting much sleep."

As if given permission, I sink back down into the high-backed recliner and let out a breath I didn't realize I was holding in and then I laugh.

"Do I look as old as I feel? I'm turning twenty-nine next week and yet I feel like I'm eighty-nine. I'm barely holding on."

Turning her attention to my uncle, she begins checking his vitals but continues speaks to me over her shoulder, her voice soft and sympathetic.

"You have more on your plate than any other twenty-eight-year-old should. You need to give yourself some slack and make plans to enjoy your big day. Maybe Josie and I could have lunch with you."

I watch as Daria slips a pressure cuff on my uncle's arm and pumps up the bulb, then slowly eases off as she checks his blood pleasure.

Josie is her seven-year-old daughter and the light of her life. When I remember to do it, I bring signed team merch to give to the adorable little girl, who once told me she wants to play hockey someday.

"Ahh, how is Josie doing? Did she end up doing her show-and-tell with the signed stick I sent her?"

Daria turns to me and smiles. "You made my girl's whole year. She couldn't stop talking about it. She named all the players from last year and said she was going to grow up to be a defenseman like her favorite player, Ballas the Beast."

At the sound of his name my heart leaps.

"That's great." My voice sounds weak, and I clear my throat surreptitiously. "No, I don't have any plans, unless you count the thousand-dollar-a-plate charity gala I'm scheduled to attend on behalf of the Spurlock family and the Vancouver Vikings." I open my phone to check my calendar, noting the time and place in my schedule. I frown knowing there won't be time to get a date. "And once again, I'm attending solo."

Daria narrows her eyes. "Why is it that a gorgeous young woman like yourself can't get a date just like that?" She snaps her fingers, then threads the stethoscope back around her neck and makes some notes in the chart next to Marv's bedside.

I snort. "Like it's that easy."

"Honey, I may have been out of the dating pool for a decade, but you've got it going on, chica." She gestures up and down toward my body. "There's not a man alive who wouldn't jump at the chance to take you to a swanky fundraiser."

Since my break-up, I've had no desire to get back on the horse, as they say, and date again. Even if I wanted to, clearly, I don't have the time to invest in a relationship. And for that matter, who would want a relationship with someone who's never around, travels weekly between two cities in two different countries, and is surrounded by professional male athletes all the time? I definitely wouldn't have time for a needy, jealous or insecure man".

When she finishes up, Daria turns to me and lifts her brows. "Wait a minute. You have plenty of men at your disposal. If it's a company-sponsored event, why not just ask one of those hot, single hockey players to be your escort? Tell them it's their duty to the team. You'd get a handsome male spec-imen on your arm for the evening and they'd get a delicious meal and get to hobnob with the rich and famous."

I give her a look. "That would be kind of awkward and weird, don't you think?"

"Girl…" She juts her hip to the side and places her fist on it in a haughty stance. "You're paying them millions a year. They can suck it up. Plus, it's not like they'd be expected to sleep with you. It's just a required public appearance for you and some company would be nice. Surely there must be one hockey player with enough brains to hold a riveting conversation for the evening?"

I suppose she has a point. Each player is required to attend a mandatory number of team functions for PR purposes throughout the year. Last year, our PR team sent several to the cancer ward at the local children's hospital, there was an event for an animal shelter, and they even found a holiday-themed Santa sleigh ride for foster kids.

A charity gala to raise funds for the heart association is part of the call. This way, I can be accompanied by someone who isn't an actual date. No potential for a romantic entanglement, No other expectations on either side beyond food and good company. Plus, icing on the cake, it would give me the opportunity to get to know one of the players a little more in depth.

The alternative of showing up alone and spending my birthday by myself is too depressing for words. Now I just need to determine who has an open schedule to attend with me. I send Christine a quick text and give her the details of what I need done.

CHRISTINE: **On it, boss.**

7

B allas

Day one of training camp is and always will be the hardest.

But today it's especially brutal.

After eighteen seasons with the league, my body is screams, *this is it*. It's the most grueling day on and off the ice I've ever experienced.

Or maybe you're just old as fuck and a fool to keep pushing yourself.

The entire roster of players, including those of us returning to the team, the new rookies, some prospects from the minor league, and a handful of hopefuls are all here this week to prove their mettle. The camp is a chance for the boys to dust off the skates after a summer of travel and downtime, and for the coaching staff and management to assess where everyone's at.

We go through fitness evaluations and full physicals, then skills evaluations led by the coaching staff. After all that, Coach Thomas divides us into two groups to break up our practice and scrimmage time on the ice and our strength training. My group is second on the ice, and I'm already sucking wind.

I have no concerns about how I'll perform with my skills or my stick work, but damn if my fitness ability and speed isn't put to the test out here. A guy my age and no longer in his prime going up against these kids who barely shave regularly is going to have it rough.

For the three-on-three, I'm teamed up with Cale, and Ax, with Soren Wolfenspiel between the pipes, his practice helmet covered with the Vikings logo and an image of a wolf with silver eyes. It seems fitting since he's very much a loner from what I hear. He's new to us this year after our previous goalie got injured and then ended up claimed off waivers to Denver.

Honestly, if they used today's skate as the sole indicator of my success on the ice this year, I just might be benched for good. At one point, right after a three-on-three scrimmage, Coach Thomas even joked about my "slow legs." Fuck me. That's rich coming from a fifty-eight-year-old. But I couldn't argue because his comment was on point and valid. Guys were skating around me like I was in the slow lane on the highway.

I toss my gear in the bins next to the equipment manager on my way into the locker rooms, wondering if I wouldn't be better off being tortured and waterboarded in a remote prison rather than going through the taxing skate and endurance trials we were put through today.

I scan the locker room to see if anyone else is out of breath or looks as beat as me. Much to my relief, I notice a few of the guys still panting and dripping with sweat so I know I'm not alone. Fortunately, we'll get a short rest after showering before we head into the team meeting room for a coaching strategy session and pep talk.

In other words, you guys suck and better work harder.

Nils Lundren, a new forward on the team, but a guy I've played against in previous seasons, pops a squat on the bench across from me. He tears off his sweat-soaked compression shirt, his chest still heaving from the workout.

"Yo, Lundy. You feeling it as much as I am?" I ask with a forced chuckle.

His eyes pop to mine and dishes it back at me in a deeply Swedish accented voice. "Not for the same reasons you are. My exhaustion is because I have a new baby who won't sleep through the night. What's your excuse?"

Laughing at the ease in his tone and good humor, I cock my thumb and finger at him. "No joke, bro. We all know I'm the decrepit one on the team."

I stand and grab my shower items, stretching to each side to get the kinks out, and wrap the towel around my waist as Nils walks at my side.

"New baby, huh? That must be hard. You got other kids?"

"Ingrid is the newborn and Elsa is our 2-year-old." Nils throws his towel up on a hook and steps into the shower stall. "The wife was not happy with the timing of our move."

I make a face. "Ouch. Yeah, that sucks. But we're glad you're here. I think we've got a solid chance."

Nils lifts his brows, turning his head over his shoulder. "As long as I can stay awake and you can keep up."

I flip him off and finish my shower.

"OKAY BOYS, settle down and let's get to it," Coach Thomas says from his platform at the front of the sloped auditorium-like conference room. "Last year was a dismal way to end the season. I know those on the team fought hard through injuries and the devasting situation with Marvin Spurlock, but this year we need to mobilize and capitalize on our God-given talents so we bring home the Cup for Vancouver. Let's go, boys. Let's do it this year!"

The room erupts with a repeating chant, *Let's go Vikes* along with some *hell, yeahs* and *let's go, boys.*

Being that I'm starting my eighteenth season, I've heard these yackity-yack, bullshit pump-you-up speeches before. It's every coach's dream to get their team to the playoffs and ultimately put the Cup on their resume. I've been lucky enough to get there several times myself and have even walked away once with a hoisting of the silver cup.

Would it be fucking awesome to win another Stanley Cup in my last year in the league? Fuck, yeah it would. But if it doesn't happen, it doesn't happen. My own personal goals are to remain healthy and finish the season with more Ws than Ls.

When the cheering dies down a bit, Coach Thomas continues, waving a hand across the room at the group of guys in front of him. "We've assembled a hell of a fucking A-team this year, thanks to our GM, Nate McGowan, and of course, our new team owner, Ms. Spurlock." He nods his chin toward the back of the room and all heads swivel around to find a scowling Nate and a smiling Karis behind us.

And fuck me, she looks incredible.

She looks sexy in her grey suit and her hair done up in some complex braid that wraps around to the back of her head and is then pinned in a tight bun at the nape.

With her hair pulled back like that, her long, slender neck is exposed. Just seeing all that warm silky skin of hers has my balls aching with the memory of slowly kissing up that throat.

I turn back around and covertly adjust myself with a tug of my pants leg. No need for anyone here to see exactly how our new owner affects me.

"If this is going to be work, then we need to push hard from the very get go, boys. No fucking around. No late nights or parties. I mean it."

Everyone groans and Nils leans over and mutters in my ear. "Says the guy who doesn't have a new baby."

Coach's eyes snaps to him. "What's that, Lundren? You got something to add?"

Nils sits up straighter, shifting uncomfortably in his chair. "No, Coach. Just agreeing with you."

"Good." He stares at him for a beat longer and then continues. "This is no party, fellas. It's eat, skate, sleep, repeat. It's going to be a daily grind. For you rookies, you're going to learn to love this process. We will have new plays to learn, skills to improve, but what it boils down to, boys, is the teamwork. That's what will get us there. Camp will be gruesome and exhausting. It will break you down and wear you out with only one goal in mind. To make every one of you champions."

With that, the room explodes in cheers and applause.

"Fuck yeah," comes a shout from a few rows ahead of me. I tip my head to see it's Tanner Rossco, a third year D-man and loud mouth. Costa, who sits behind him, slaps him on the back, whether for encouragement or to shut him up, who knows?

Coach goes on for a few more minutes, checking his notes to point out the things he noticed during the scrimmages, then finishes up with the passing of the baton.

"And now I'm going to hand this over to our esteemed owner, Ms. Spurlock, who has something she wants to discuss with all of you."

A silent hush descends over the room as Coach moves out from the platform and Karis gracefully strides down the aisle to the front to take his place.

There's not one pair of eyes that isn't laser-focused on our beautiful club owner. I know what these boys are thinking and can guarantee you there's some lewd scenarios being imagined amongst these guys, too. I just hope no one is stupid enough to say something.

I will take down any guy who mutters an inappropriate word.

Karis stands poised, if not a little stiff and cool. She's tall and slender with shapely round curves in her hips and thighs. Her delicate fingers wrap tightly on each side of the podium and the plump shape of her breasts can be seen as she leans forward with intention. She clears her throat.

I clear my thoughts.

"Gentleman, welcome to training camp. On behalf of the leadership staff and ownership group, including my uncle, Marv, we're looking forward to a great year ahead. As you may know, my uncle is still unwell, and therefore I've taken over the ownership duties until he is back on his feet." Her breath stalls for a beat and I see the sadness flicker in her green eyes. She drops a hand to the tablet she placed on the podium.

There have been no reports or updates in the media or from the team public relations group on the status of Marv's condition. All we know is he's back home in Seattle recovering while Karis is now in charge. "Many of the duties of ownership, aside from making sure the club is financially stable, entail public endeavors. Which leads me to this PR request for a few of you."

The entire room grows silent and seems to shrink in size. A glance around me tells me exactly what they're doing. The guys slink down in their seats in an effort to make themselves appear small and inconspicuous, hoping to avoid being a target.

Karis opens up her tablet, scanning the content before she

lifts her head and her eyes peruse the room, seemingly looking for all the players on her list.

"The Vikings organization is an integral part of this community, and as such, we must show up and give back to those who support us. Several events are scheduled prior to the season start. You've all received and responded to my assistant already, who reached out to each of you to confirm your schedule availability and the events you'd be interested in attending. I have a list of those who will be required to attend which events as a representative of the Vikings."

She begins reading off event names, dates, and each player she'd like in attendance. My name is called last.

"Ballas Keeney," she says, her eyes pinning me with a look that's a cross between a demand and a plea. "You'll be attending the Vancouver Fights Heart Disease event this Friday evening in honor of my uncle and all those who suffer from the disease."

Fuck. I mentally try to devise an excuse to get out of this event, but I know it's of no use. Obviously, she knows I'm not doing anything and have no other plans but icing my sore muscles after a full week of camp. I simply nod in understanding. Next to me, Nils snickers, elbowing me in the ribs in jest.

"The one time having a newborn gives me an advantage."

I hold out my fist for him to bump it. "At least I get free dinner and drinks." Nils groans and slumps back in his seat.

"Does anyone have any questions?" Karis asks politely, her eyes scanning over the room.

Dieter Volmer, a fairly seasoned guy and backup goalie, raises his hand. "Uh, does the event we're going to include a seat for my spouse?"

Someone in the back snickers. "Whipped!"

Karis smiles graciously. "Of course. For those of you who would like to bring a plus-one, you may. Just let me know or contact my admin, Christine, so we can have a ticket ready. For those who will be solo attendees, you're more than welcome to attend with me."

You can hear a puck drop in Pittsburgh for as quiet as it gets. That's when I hear it. A nasty under-his-breath comment from a 19-year-old prospect sitting behind me who thinks it's funny to be disrespectful of our female owner of the team.

"Oooh...a wine, dine, and sixty-nine event." The kid chuckles. "I'd like to raise the paddle to that ass."

It might be jealousy tearing through me like a breakaway down the ice, but I'm fuming hot with rage when I swing my arm around to rest it on the back of my chair and glare at the punk ass. He smirks because he thinks he's hot shit.

"Fucking shut your mouth, prospect, and have some fucking respect." I murmur, then growl like the savage beast I am and narrow my eyes in icy censure. "Remember she's the one who can either pay your salary or trade your ass to wherever the hell she wants. Got it?"

The kid goes pale, his jaw falling open at the severity of my death stare. He nods and swallows noticeably.

Karis continues, none the wiser to this punk's remarks. "Thank you to those who will be joining me as leaders of our team. Those players I called should expect to receive an email tomorrow with all the details. If you have any other questions, my door is always open. I look forward to seeing you all out on the ice this week and good luck."

There's a sigh of relief from the guys who didn't get selected and everyone claps as Karis steps off the small platform and walks back down the aisle with a graceful stride.

I turn in my seat to find Nils giving me a curious look.

I shrug. "What? I'm just being a leader like coach asked, eh?"

8

K aris – Las Vegas Last December

"Bend over, spread your legs, and let me see that delicious pussy of yours."

I do as Ballas commands, his voice brooking no objection from me. I place my feet out in a wide V-shape and bend in half over the king-sized bed, my arms outstretched.

"That's a good girl. Now hold on and don't move because I'm going to eat your pussy until you are hoarse from screaming with pleasure."

The filthy words he uses send zings of sexual bliss to all the right places where I ache for him. Even though this is the third time he's taken me tonight, I can't get enough. I've reveled each time over his remarkable sexual endurance and virility. Ballas knows how to please a woman with his low and raspy directives and every patient touch and each seductive kiss.

It's as if he's savoring me like he would a strong cocktail—slow and intentional.

You'd think I'd have had enough by this point, but my body still quivers at the very thought of his lips and mouth kissing me in that forbidden place where I'm so wet for him. Where I'm ready to have his fingers and cock sinking in deep inside me to get me off to that next orgasm, each one bigger and more intense with pleasure than the last.

"Ballas," I moan, my eyes half-shut with arousal and my breath coming out in fast pants as my fingernails dig into the bedsheets. His feathery touch flutters over my clit and then through my wet folds. I buck against him, wanting him to stop the teasing and torment and give me what I want. He chuckles coolly, completely unaffected by my needy desire.

"Greedy little princess, aren't you?"

Then his fingers begin to move—but not around my pulsing clit or into my wet entrance. They leave my sex and climb upward above my tailbone. He gently rolls a thumb along the length of my spine, caressing over the puckered skin of my scar. I stiffen and try to flip over to put a stop to his curious perusal, but Ballas's strength is no match for mine. He grips my hips firmly in his grasp and holds me in place. I clench my teeth and cringe knowing exactly what he sees and feels under his touch. My disfigured body is an embarrassment, something so ugly I want to disappear under the covers and hide from his scrutiny.

I am completed naked and exposed to him and at his mercy. There is no doubt that in a few seconds, he'll want to leave after getting an eyeful of the ugly, raised, puckered, reddish brown scar; the reminder of my pain that snakes down the middle of my back and looks like a science experiment gone bad.

"I'm sorry." I squirm loose from his hold, tears pricking at the back of my eyes. I want to get up and leave and avoid the awkward conversation that's sure to follow. I turn away on my hip and drop my head down to hide from his gaze. "I know it's grotesque. I can lay on my back so you don't have to see it."

I plant my butt down on the edge of the bed, suddenly cold and vulnerable under the awkwardness of this situation. For a long moment, it's silent. Ballas remains standing at the end of the bed while my eyes remain cast downward so all I see is his feet.

When I finally get the courage to lift my head, his expression is indecipherable. Did he lose his arousal and interest in me because of this imperfection on my skin?

Is he going to ask me to put my clothes back on?

Or worse, is he going to call it a night and leave?

"I'll understand if you want to go. My ex said it was ugly and distracting in bed," I hiccup a choked sob. "He called me unfuckable. It's why he said he slept with other women and cheated on me."

"Jesus fucking Christ."

It's not the worst thing a man has ever done. Sex with Bradley was usually with lights off and fully clothed so he would avoid touching it when we were intimate.

But that's not what Ballas does.

Instead of confirming my worst fears and doing exactly what Bradley did, Ballas sits down beside me and reaches for my hand. Slipping his fingers through mine, he lifts our joined hands to his temple, guiding my index finger over the crevice-shaped scar at his forehead. The small indentation was hidden by his overgrown hair that he pushes out of the way.

"Do you feel this?"

I tip my gaze up and nod. "Yes."

"And how about this one?" He raises his chin to indicate the scar hidden underneath, where stubble refuses to grow any longer.

I shrug. "Okay."

He smirks. "Oh, and don't forget this doozy…"

He bends over at the waist, running our hands up his left kneecap where a nice long scar is evident from some sort of knee surgery.

"Your point?"

Ballas straightens, keeping my hand in his, but furrows his brows at me. "The point I'm trying to make is that I have multiple scars on my body, yet you haven't gotten all squeamish about them and you haven't thought they made me too grotesque to fuck, right?"

I let out a small laugh, waving my other hand over his impeccable body. "What you're packing makes it very hard to notice your small, insignificant scars."

Ballas lays me back with a gentle press of his palm over my collarbone. I go willingly. He leans down and props himself on his elbow at my side. Now facing one another, mouths just inches apart, he trails a fingertip between my breasts, circling over each nipple, which pucker instantly. He continues the sensual path down to my belly button and I can no longer think straight.

His eyes sweep over my breasts, lingering at my middle in an admiring gaze. "You are beautiful, Karis. Our scars are what make us unique but don't need to define us. Each one holds a story behind it that made us who we are today." The heat of his body begins to light the fire that was just extinguished by my own self-conscious behavior, and his sweet words are more than I would have ever expected to hear come from a man known as the Beast.

This is not the way I thought our night together would go. I thought he'd fuck me once, maybe stay for a drink, then be on his way. That would be that. I hadn't asked him up here for a lesson in loving my body, scars and all.

He settles his weight on top of me, his hips rolling between my thighs. Even with the interruption my embarrassment provided, Ballas is still hard and throbbing against my center. I trace my fingertip over the slopes of his shoulders and then run my thumb over the scar at his temple.

"That's sweet of you to say, but the notable difference is that you're a hockey player, Ballas. Injuries and scars come with the territory and are kind of part of the job. Scars makes you look rugged and tough."

I cup his chiseled face in my palm and slide it over the generous curve of his shoulders, down the planes of his muscular back until I land on his round hockey butt. My God, what a perfect ass he has. He smirks as he rolls forward, sliding his cock over my mound, drawing out a mewl from my mouth.

The corners of his mouth quirk up. "Did you just call me sweet?"

I can't help the snort that pops out. "And if I did? What would you do about it?"

He snarls and I suddenly find myself on top of him. I draw up my legs to straddle his bulging thighs, which aren't the only body part that bulges underneath me. His hard erection wedges once again between my legs, connecting with my sensitive clit. I suck in a short breath and dig my knees into his sides. Then I anchor my hold onto his shoulders for leverage and give an experimental rock of my hips forward.

What freaked me out moments ago now has me panting with desire as Ballas smooths his thumb down the middle of my back again. Over and over the puckered flesh. This time the sensation travels straight to my pussy and my inner walls clench with a furious need for him to bury himself inside.

"Karis, let me make something perfectly clear," he murmurs, lifting his head to suckle at my nipple, placing hot searing kisses over the globes of my breasts. "You are fucking sexy as hell. Your ex is a shallow fucking asshole who is completely unworthy of you. And you are not the reason he cheated. He cheated because he's a cheat. And the things I'm going to do to you are anything but sweet."

God, I didn't expect Ballas to be both tender and filthy at the same time.

Truthfully, I'm glad tonight is just a one-time thing and we won't ever have to see each other again. I just hope he won't walk away from this night and remember me as some lame-ass blubbering girl who cried like a baby over her ex-boyfriend's verbal abuse.

All those thoughts are quickly shoved away when he picks up the packaged condom from the side table, rips it open with his teeth and slides it over his erect cock. He kisses my mouth one more time and then lines up at my entrance.

Looking me dead in the eye, he circles my waist in his big hands and thrusts inside.

"Now be a good girl and fucking ride me hard."

"Karis? There's someone here to see you."

Christine's voice pulls me out of my NSFW inappropriate revery from that night in bed with Ballas. One look at my face that's flushed with the heat of lust and she's going to think something's wrong with me. And there is something wrong...I just had a very sexy and panty-soaking daydream about Ballas, the man I can't stop thinking about no matter how hard I try.

I shift in my chair uncomfortably and realize my panties are damp. Great. How am I supposed to act like a professional when all I want to do is slip my hand down my skirt and finger myself to the memory of the dirty-talking beast?

I clear my throat and reach for my water glass, taking a long drink from it to quench my thirst before I respond.

"Sure, send them in," I croak, straightening in my chair and taking a deep breath to calm my rapid heart rate. "Who is it?"

Assuming it's Nate or a staff member needing to talk through a financial solution with me, I grab a few of my favorite red Skittles from my candy dish and pop them in my mouth, only to have one get lodged on the way down. I nearly choke when Christine answers my question.

"It's Ballas Keeney."

9

Ballas

Christine smiles politely when she turns around, opens the door wider, and ushers me into Karis's office.

Karis looks up from her desk, sputtering and coughing like she just swallowed something. A deep scarlet blooms across her cheeks.

"Oh my goodness, are you okay, boss?" Christine asks, rushing to Karis's side to dutifully hand her some water. Karis accepts the glass from her assistant with eyes closed.

"Are you choking?" I ask, a little worried as the coughing fit continues. "Do I need to perform mouth-to-mouth?"

Karis's eyes pop open wide and she shakes her head frantically, holding up her hand and gesturing for a moment. Finally, when the coughing subsides, she takes a sip of water, pounding on her chest and clearing her throat.

"Woo. I'm fine now. Thanks Christine." She slams the remaining water and hands the glass back over to her assistant. Christine walks over to the mini bar and opens the door before turning back toward me. "Would you care for something to drink, Ballas? Water? Pellegrino? Or maybe a coconut water?"

Karis wipes away the tears that had spilled from her eyes during her coughing fit with a tissue and tosses it toward the waste basket, missing completely because her gaze is now glued to her laptop screen.

I shake my head and bend down to pick up Karis's missed shot, tossing it in the basket at the side of Karis's desk. "No, thank you. This will only take a sec."

She shuts the fridge door and straightens, placing a carton of coconut water on Karis's desk and waits for a dismissal. Karis flicks her gaze toward Christine and smiles. God, that smile is perfection and hits me in the solar plexus.

"Please let my next appointment know I'm running a bit behind." Karis finally raises her eyes and pins me with a stare. "What can I do for you, Ballas?"

Oh, if only I could thoroughly answer that question with exactly what I've been thinking but indulging those thoughts won't get me anywhere.

"You tell me." I shrug, waiting for Christine to shut the door behind her as she exits the office. "You asked me to come to you with any questions about this gala. So here I am. In need of answers." I gesture with the wave of my hands down my torso like I'm showing off the prize car on a game show.

"You could have just emailed or asked Christine about scheduling."

I snort, checking over my shoulder that we're alone. "And miss out on the chance to do the Heimlich or possible mouth-to-mouth on you? No way. I'm here to help."

Karis rolls her eyes. "As you can see, I'm just fine and don't need the help of your mouth."

That flush that had diminished slightly over her face comes roaring back to life the moment she realizes what she's said and how it sounds.

HMM...SO she is thinking about my mouth.

"So, you say...but I seem to recall this mouth of mine assisted you on previous occasions. Who knows, maybe you'll have need additional assistance at the event?"

By the way she inhales sharply, I know she knows exactly what I'm referring to. This is a deal or no deal time. Karis will either try to ignore the chemistry between us and rescind my invite to the fundraiser, deciding to keep her professional distance. Or she won't, leaving room for a potential repeat.

I take a seat, and lean forward, my elbows on my thighs. Karis digs through her candy dish and plucks out a few Skittles, tossing them in her mouth one by one. My gaze narrows on her lips. I bet she'd taste so sweet right now. Sex and candy flavored.

Fuck, I admonish myself for going there.

The truth is, I came in here to tell her I wasn't going to attend and she'd have to find someone else to go. I only have so much self-discipline and that's wearing thing. if I'm made to attend this event with Karis, it won't be easy to hold back. I'll want to relive those moments we shared in Vegas. I'll want to know if she's still wet for me every time she's around me, just as I'm hard for her.

Plus, Karis has made it abundantly clear to me exactly how she feels and I can't imagine she really wants me to attend the event with her anyway. Why would she?

"I actually came up to tell you I'm not going to this event."

Karis blanches as if rebuffed and straightens in her chair. "What? Why?"

I give her a look that says, '*you know why.*' She crosses her arms defensively in front of her chest, her mouth set in annoyance as she straightens her shoulders.

"It's a requirement, Ballas. You can't just not go because you don't want to." Then her expression shifts slightly along with the set of her shoulders. "What are you, like twelve? You don't think you can keep your dick in your pants for a few hours?"

My voice deepens to a husky murmur. "Not around you."

"Don't flatter yourself, Ballas," she scoffs. "This is not a date and I haven't asked you to go out on. I'm certainly not interested in a repeat of..." Her face heats again and she glances away like she's searching for the words and frustrated over them. "This is a business event. I expect you to act professionally and accordingly."

I chuckle dryly. "Oh, it's not me I'm worried about."

She huffs out an annoyed breath. "Excuse me? It wasn't me who initiated that kiss," she snaps, pointing toward the exact spot where I kissed her the last time I was in her office. The day I overstepped and broke my own rules to get her out of my system. Obviously, that didn't work out to my advantage. "That was all on you."

I straighten in my chair and nod in agreement. "Yep, you're right. I have no excuse for my behavior that day. But I promise you, my focus now is on the season ahead. So you don't have to worry. I won't—"

"You won't what?" she asks almost breathlessly, her voice a soft murmur as something flickers in the back of her eyes. I notice her throat constrict as she swallows and she bites down on the corner of her lip.

That's a good question. Why can't I get over this attraction to Karis? My desire for this woman—*my boss*—has yet to diminish and I still want her.

It's been well over nine months since Vegas and three months since I last kissed her, yet it's all still fresh in my mind. Her taste. Her scent. Her moans that go straight to my cock when I touch her. The way I *want* to touch her even right now as she shoots darts at me with her eyes.

Which is exactly why I shouldn't attend this gala with her.

It's risky to spend time with Karis at a function outside the confines of the arena. It might easily strain and snap the tenuous strands of my self-control.

My mouth twitches with amusement. "I won't do anything you don't ask me to do."

Karis flusters and her expression morphs to something unreadable. Before she drops her gaze to her watch, I think I see challenge.

"Good. Thank you. What I want is for you to leave now." She dismisses me with a nod. "Christine will give you the details for Friday's event."

She pauses, staring at my hair and motioning at it with the twirl of her index finger. "And if you can, please do something with that mop of yours."

"What's wrong with my salad?" I bark in laughter, running a hand through my unruly, very shaggy hair that I let grow out this summer. "You can't underestimate the value of the hockey flow."

Karis rolls her eyes with a sigh. "Fine, whatever. Just look presentable, please. I mean, you're representing our team."

"I've been to a charity fundraiser before, Karis. I'm sure I can manage to look respectable enough for you." I stand and give her a salute, lifting my brows. "I can even act respectably."

"Promises, promises."

I just hope it's one I can keep.

"Nice one, Keeners!" Nils calls out from behind me as I give a no-look pass over to Costa, who then launches a one-handed chip to the back of the net, the puck sailing just over the outstretched hand of Wolf.

Wolf smacks the end of his stick on the ice in front of him with a loud growl. Seems fitting, considering his name.

"Atta boy, Costa," I cheer. I stop in front of my scrimmage partner and tap the top of his helmet, then skate in front of the slot and give Soren a tap on his shoulder pad. "Sorry, Wolfie. Better now than when it really counts, eh?"

Soren's eyes shoot daggers at me as he flips his mask to the top of his head and grabs for the plastic water bottle sitting on the net. He takes a giant swig before dousing his head with it.

"I should've had that fucker."

"I wouldn't worry about it, Wolf," Cale shouts over his shoulder at our goalie, a smile splitting wide across his bearded cheeks. "You'll move up from the Peewees soon enough."

We laugh at the insult and Wolf's corresponding *fuck you, Cost,'* and skate off to the bench as the next shift takes the ice. Today's our final day of camp and after our day off tomorrow, we'll have our first preseason game on Saturday against Toronto. Thankfully, it's on home ice so we don't have to travel, which is a good thing because the charity event I've been ordered to attend is tomorrow night. I want to get a good night's sleep after that so I can be rested and ready for battle on Saturday night.

We normally take things pretty easy on the preseason games, the purpose to identify where our holes are in our defensive lines, work out some of the plays we've practiced during the training camp and the prospects showing what they got in hopes of gaining a spot on the roster.

I join the bench, grab some water, and watch as the next group of guys battle it out in front of us. A strange feeling of nostalgia washes over me, followed by a moment of profound sadness, as I realize that this will be my final day of training camp ever.

This could be it. That's all she wrote. I may never have this moment again.

My entire career flashes before my eyes as I watch our number one draft pick this season rookie, Shaw Benning, who has already demonstrated that he's everything he's been touted to be. A sensational player who has all the drive and talent that I had when I started my career a million years ago.

I consider all that I've done in these past eighteen seasons—the wins, the losses, the struggles to overcome injuries, the work I put into outsmarting and outskating my opponents, the championship highs, the crushing lows.

Do I have anything to show for all of it now?

There's my championship ring from the year I played on the Stanley Cup winning team. I'll have won the Norris a couple of times. I may even have my number retired with the Vikings.

But outside of hockey? I've got nothing to show for my life, no personal attachments and no one waiting in the wings once I retire.

My stomach fills with a dread I've only felt once before.

And there is fuck all I can do about it now.

10

———

K aris

The fundraiser starts at 6 p.m. with an open bar, which gave me plenty of time to have my hair, makeup, and nails done after leaving the office at three.

Christine wanted me to indulge in some extra extravagant beauty regimen since it's my birthday, after all.

"If a girl can't splurge on her birthday and not feel guilty about it, when can she?" she'd wisely said when I put up a fuss over the unnecessary treatment.

The guilt, however, comes from the fact that I won't get a chance to fly down to Seattle this weekend to check in on Marv. With tonight's event and the game against Toronto tomorrow night, my schedule won't allow me the time.

I did, however, FaceTime with him for a few minutes while I waited for my hair color to process. The nurse on duty, Geneva, is a sweet woman who always offers a kind smile and words of positivity. She held the phone at Marv's bedside so he could hear my voice as I spoke with him and filled him in on how everything is going.

It never fails to choke me up when I talk to Marv. I can't help wondering if I'm doing the right thing.

All the doctors I've consulted with have offered conflicting opinions on the status of his medical condition and whether he will ever come out of this coma. One, Dr. Shikary, a soft-spoken doctor with an even better bedside manner did at least offer me some hope with a therapy she recommended.

"I know it's a difficult position to be in, Ms. Spurlock, and at times it feels useless." The doctor gently laid her hand over mine and smiled. "By employing these simple activities associated with the coma stimulation program, you may help in the overall recovery. His brain may not function in a responsive way, but it gives you something constructive to do."

I grapple with what to do on a daily, if not hourly, basis. There are people out there who believe Marv will never pull through. And even if he does, I know his long-term cognitive and physical functions could be severely impacted.

But I won't give up on him. Marv was there by my side after accident nearly fifteen years ago, gave me hope when there was little for me to hold on to after the accident. He guided me through the toughest part of my life. He may not have showered me with love or physical affection, but what he offered was just as valuable.

That's why I won't give up on him when the going gets tough. He's all I have to hang on to in this world.

I won't lose you, too, Marv.

I stare down at the dress I picked out for tonight. It's a floor-length, black-sequined dress that shimmers when it catches light. I stare at my reflection in the mirror in my closet, 1940s music playing softly in the background because it's Marv's favorite, and I wonder who it is that I'm looking at.

A girl who had to grow up too fast after losing her parents. A girl who couldn't walk for months after multiple surgeries to fuse her spine back together. And a now fully grown woman who went through grad school, took ownership of a basketball team, learned the ropes of managing a franchise in a sport she knew nothing about, and turned it into a championship team.

That very same woman who reluctantly stepped into her uncle's shoes as his successor and taken over everything, alone and on her own.

I try to smile at the woman in the mirror and focus on the positive and all I've accomplished, hoping to instill a belief in myself because Marv isn't here to bolster me up. Questions swim in my head about what my purpose is and if this is what I want to be doing this time next year. Or five years from now.

Is it what I truly want?

Marv guided me into a life and a direction that may not have been mine if my parents had survived.

Today I turn twenty-nine. Back in my teens, I thought I'd be married and have started a family before my thirties. In the next decade, will I continue down this lonely road, follow in my uncle's footsteps as a billionaire with no family and no special relationship?

My thoughts are interrupted with the ping of my phone. I glance over at the island in the middle of my closet where my phone sits and see it's a text from my ride. The event is on the other side of Vancouver and I wanted to indulge in some champagne tonight, so I hired a driver to shuttle me to and from.

I grab my phone and stick it in my clutch, then take one final assessment of myself, lifting my chin up and my shoulders back to practice the art of appearing confident and happy.

Even if I feel as from that reality as I am from the moon.

"YOU LOOK ABSOLUTELY STUNNING, KARIS."

I accept the compliment from Diana Thorpe with a hug. Diana is the wife of the head of St. Luke's Hospital's children's heart center. I've only met her once before, but I like her warmth and genuine friendliness. She's the real deal in a world full of fakes.

I smile when I move out of her arms. "So do you, Diana. As always."

She waves away my returned sentiment, as if I'm a fool to think so. If I had to guess, I'd say she's in her mid-fifties. Diana is as petite as she is worldly, an extreme athlete who hikes and skis all over the globe. When not traipsing up and down mountains Diana also serves as the head of an organization that works with impoverished children in developing nations.

Her fire and tenacity for life is something I would like to bottle up and use for myself. I aspire to be more like her and wish I had even an ounce of the courage she does to handle all the challenges that come her way.

Her warm gaze moves behind me and scans the room.

"Where's your date for the evening?" she inquires when her eyes land back on me. "What fool of a man would leave a beautiful woman like yourself unattended even for a moment?"

I lift my eyebrows, draw a sip of champagne from the flute, and chuckle. "No date for me tonight. Unless you count a table full of hockey-playing brutes."

Diana laughs leans in conspiratorially. "Let's trade. Your brutes for a table of boring doctors and researchers."

We laugh as she clinks my glass with hers in a toast and begin to talk over the music and voices that fill the space within the large ballroom. I try to keep my interest on our lively discussion about her travels, but my gaze has been keenly focused on the open doors of the ballroom, watching for one man in particular to appear.

God, I'm hopeless.

I made it very clear to Ballas that this was not a date. I even pointed out his tousled hair and made a big deal out of him doing something with it, only because I find it to be one of the most devastatingly distracting features on him. His hair is a wave of disheveled sex appeal. I want to lace my fingers through the soft strands, bury my nose in his neck, and inhale that spicy, smoky scent of him.

"Now tell me, dear. How are things going with the hockey team?" Diana asks, drawing my attention back to her. "I have to say, I don't have much interest in sports, but Gordon roots for the Vikings and even has season tickets. Personally, I prefer the ballet."

I smile and give her a conspiratorial wink. "I have to admit, even I sometimes prefer the performing arts over sports myself, but I fear I don't have a choice any longer. Although I have grown a fonder appreciation for it now that I realize how hard these guys work and their athleticism."

Diana's eyes wonder toward the bar, landing on a group of athletes and local celebrities. I follow her gaze and scan the mix of attendees in search of Ballas.

"Ah yes," she says with an admiring gaze. "Their athleticism certainly is a plus."

She tears her eyes away and gives me a wink. I return it with a smile of appreciation.

"If I don't get a chance to talk with Gordon tonight, please let him know how much I appreciate his loyal support of the Vikings. I know I wasn't interested in them until…" I let my words trail off, the implication of my unspoken thought obvious.

With a pat on my arm, Diana gives me a sympathetic smile, her eyes now glittering with tears.

"Oh, my dear. I can't tell you how sorry we are about your uncle Marvin. He and Gordon aren't terribly close, but I do know Gordon has kept tabs on Marv's situation through his circle of friends. Has there been any improvement in his condition?"

I shake my head and blink away the tears that I promised I wouldn't shed tonight. It's just so lonely celebrating a birthday without the one person in my life who has made every one of my previous birthdays special.

While Marv has never been overly affectionate with me—often distant with his head always on his businesses matters—I still knew he cared. Maybe that's the reason I appear overly cool and distant to people until they get to know me. I'm not oblivious to the rumors I've heard and the ice queen label I've been given. Marv taught me to portray myself as no nonsense and no bullshit. But I do have a heart and I'm not incapable of giving and showing love and affection.

I crave it, too. I want a man who will be there to support me with his strength so I can let go. I don't need flowers and candy or a ballroom full of balloons on my birthday.

I just want someone to make me feel cherished and loved.

I finish my drink and set it down on the high table next to us as I consider the best way to explain Marv's status. "Marv is stable. I've moved him out of the rehab center and back into his home with 24-hour care. He still remains unconscious and in a coma, hooked up to a ventilator and feeding tube. I'm probably just holding out hope he'll regain consciousness. It's my only birthday wish."

Diana's expression moves from sadness to excitement, her smile turning bright. "It's your birthday today?"

I shrug. "Yep. I'm celebrating my last year in my twenties."

"Oh, you young thing. What I wouldn't give for my twenties again."

Then, if possible, Diana's smile grows even wider as her gaze moves behind me. When I turn to look over my shoulder, I'm met with broad shoulders in a black tuxedo.

Ballas stands there, two glasses in his hands. One is a tumbler with a dark amber liquid and the other is a champagne flute. His magnetism is potent and my heart lurches wildly at how handsome he looks in the tux.

He offers the flute to me, the corners of his mouth tipped up underneath his trim beard. His hair is neatly slicked back from his face and his eyes offer a glint of promises.

"You looked in need of a drink."

Did Diana just swoon?

I accept the offered glass. "Thank you, Ballas. That's very thoughtful."

Ballas raises his hand and tips his glass to the edge of mine. "Think nothing of it. It's the least I can do, especially now that I hear it's your birthday."

"Thanks." I try to keep the blush from creeping up my face, but it's no use. Ballas has a way of making the heat rise unbidden in my body. And not just in my cheeks. "Let's not make a big deal of it. In fact, let's just keep it between us."

The smirk he gives me tells me exactly what he's thinking.

"I'm good with secrets." He winks.

Goddamn him for being so hot.

Realizing Diana is quietly observing the exchange between us, I spin back to her and champagne spills out over the top of my glass. I swipe my finger over the rim and bring the liquid to my lips, licking it off. A low, audible noise comes from Ballas's throat.

"Diana, forgive me for being so rude. Let me introduce you to—"

"Ballas the Beast."

My eyes widen at Diana's declaration. "You just said you don't watch hockey."

Diana laughs and waves her hand. "I don't. But one doesn't have to be a hockey fan in this town to know who Ballas Keeney is. I'm so happy to see you again, Ballas."

He bends at the waist, raises Diana's hand to his lips, and kisses her knuckles. Good Lord, this man is the true definition of lady's man. *Flirtatious player, more like it.*

"Nice to see you again, Mrs. Thorpe."

"Assuming you have no other commitments tonight," Diana prods, grabbing onto one of Ballas's hands. "I think you should act as Karis's escort for the evening and be her birthday date."

I nearly choke on my champagne.

My eyes snap up to Ballas, who gives me a crooked grin.

"I'm happy to help with that. Consider it done."

11

Ballas

"How do you know Diana Thorpe?"

I chuckle at Karis's question and reach for the breadbasket in front of us on the table, offering a roll to her before taking one for myself.

"This ain't my first rodeo with charity events." I grab a pat of butter and slather some on my roll, watching Karis out of the corner of my eye. She takes a small bite of the bread and places it back down on her plate. "We get called on a lot, as you know, to attend these shindigs. I met Dr. and Mrs. Thorpe at an event last year to help war refugees."

The expression on Karis's face softens, like the walls around her begin to fall and crumble. But it could just be my imagination hoping she won't keep up the hardened exterior around me. She brushes the sleeve of my dinner jacket when she reaches for her drink, and the heat scores through my arm like I've been branded.

Fuck, I'm not sure how she continues to stir me up when there is nothing that could ever come of it.

Just the way I like it.

No commitments. No ties. No relationships.

This attraction should've stayed in Vegas where it belongs. Yet here I am, sitting next to her in this ballroom dinner table, surrounded by her sweet and tantalizing scent that does unspeakable things to my body. Things I shouldn't be considering doing to her.

Like licking her hot pussy until she writhes in pleasure against my mouth.

As if she knows exactly where my imagination has gone, her gaze climbs up my torso and over my face, her eyes flashing something dark and unreadable when they meet mine. I glide a hand over my beard and lift my brows in response.

There's no way she could possibly be thinking what I am. She made it clear nothing was to happen between us. Period. End of story.

I promised I'd be good.

But just like in hockey, leads can change with the sudden slap of a stick and the lightning-fast redirection of a puck.

The rest of the fundraising event is filled with auctioning off magnum wine bottles, trips to Turks and Caicos, luxury spa days, and even the dessert trays on each table. I've been keeping my hands busy with folding a cocktail napkin into an origami swan, something I learned years ago from a kid in juniors.

It's then that the auctioneer calls up a special guest in the audience.

"And now ladies and gentlemen, we've received a very generous gift from our very own Karis Spurlock. Karis, come on up and tell us what you've donated."

Karis slides out of her chair and makes her way up the stage, smiling brightly and hugging Gordon and Diana Thorpe, who have also joined her at the front. The auctioneer hands the microphone to Karis.

"Good evening, ladies and gentlemen. It's an honor to be here tonight in support of this great cause. I know that my uncle, Marv, has been a very big supporter of the work done by this organization led by Dr. and Mrs. Thorpe. As a tribute to my uncle and on behalf of the Vancouver Vikings, I am donating a suite for one of our home games."

The auctioneer raises a paddle to the screen behind the stage where a video clip is shown of a home game from last season.

The montage starts with a clip of me scoring a goal against Dallas. It's one of my personal career highlights because just seconds before I'd received a pass from Costa and then deked the puck around Sergei Russo, the asshole to beat all assholes and the one guy in the league I can't stand.

The audience in the ballroom watches as the crowd in the video erupts in crazed.

Karis continues once the clip finishes, her gaze finding mine with a knowing smile. "And to add to this already amazing package, how about we see if one of our players in attendance tonight would be willing to add in something extra? Ballas and Brett, can you both please stand?"

I give a disgruntled glance over to my teammate and other d-man on the team, Brett Cannfield, who sits with his arm over his wife Jeanette's shoulder. He groans and bobs his chin down to his chest in a resigned manner as his wife gives him a friendly nudge in the ribs.

"I had a feeling we'd be getting roped into something more than just showing up tonight." He begins to stand up, adjusting his gray suit jacket, but I wave at him to sit back down.

Cannfield is one of the least social adults and biggest introverts I know. To get him to say two words on the ice or even in the locker room is like pulling teeth, and that's saying a lot since he's missing two of his teeth already. My teammate looks absolutely tormented at the idea of having to get up on stage, so I do my duty as a defenseman and protect the goal.

In this case, the goal happens to be Canners.

All eyes in the room are currently on us so I now gesture with both hands for him to sit back down.

"I've got this, bro. Sit back and have some more wine."

The room fills with applause, whistles, and chants of, "Let's go, Vikings," to encourage me on as Karis beckons me to the stage with a crook of her finger.

That's all it takes to fill my head with images of her standing naked in a hotel room, seductively summoning me with that bent finger until I stand in front of her and run my hands over her slender body.

I shake my thoughts free and head up to the stage.

I'm not crowd-shy or hesitant in front of an audience like some of my teammates. No, I don't always like the attention of the media when I've played like shit, but up here like this? This is just for fun and to raise money for a good cause.

I step up next to her and cover the mic in her hand with my palm. I bend down so my mouth is next to Karis's ear, breathing in her fragrant scent, and I whisper my intentions.

"You owe me. I intend to collect later."

She pulls away and snaps a widened gaze up to mine. I smile innocently and turn my attention to the well-fed and glassy eyed drunken crowd of hockey-loving people to give them a show so they'll fork over their money.

"What'll it be?" I ask, speaking into the mic. "Dinner with me and my signed jersey after a home practice this season? Or..." I shimmy my shoulders and pull slightly at my tie. "A striptease?"

This gets the audience laughing and cheering even louder. Fred, the auctioneer, gets into the act and steps in front of me, waving his hands like he's trying to stop me from going too far.

"Whoa, whoa, whoa! This is a family event, Ballas!" He laughs and then raises the paddle. "Okay, folks, who'll start the bidding at $1000 for dinner—fully clothed, I will remind you—with Vikings hockey player Number 18, Ballas *'The Beast'* Keeney?"

I throw an arm over Fred and shake my head at the crowd. "Come on, Fred. Let them have a little fun, eh? Who wants to see me strip nekkid?"

That gets the crowd amped up even furthers and after a fast-paced and rather hilarious bidding war, when the auctioneer has called the final bid, I've helped raise nearly ten grand for the cause. Not bad for an old veteran like me.

I still got it.

Now I just need to figure out how to collect my payback from Karis.

12

K aris

"Excuse me. I'll be right back."

My announcement is made to the few guests still at the table right now.

Brett and his wife have gone home to relieve their babysitter, having fulfilled the obligation to the team by attending the event tonight. Lesson learned on knowing your players and their personalities. It never even occurred to me to check and see if a professional hockey player might have severe anxiety and a strong aversion to being the spotlight. I figured that, since they play a sport in front of thousands of fans, the few hundred in tonight's audience would be a walk in the park.

Ballas had cupped my elbow as he led me down the stairs as we exited the stage, and I asked him why Cannfield hadn't joined him.

"You should really ask him," Ballas said in a low, almost reproachful tone. "But next time, you should really ask your PR team some specifics and vet each player more carefully before requiring their participation in front of an audience."

That comment still stabs at my conscience as I grab the rhinestone-encrusted clutch that had once belonged to my mother from the table and head toward ballroom doors. My intention is to steal a moment away from the crowd to catch my breath and slow my racing heart.

You owe me.

Those whispered words Ballas said to me on stage keep running through my head. It was a secret thrill, etched softly in the recesses of his voice, filtered through Ballas's lips to my ear. A reminder that his reward would need to be repaid.

Now I need to keep myself from flipping through ideas about Ballas's plans to collect.

Dammit. Why does he make me run so hot and cold?

One minute I insist he stop flirting with me. The next I'm practically begging him to do it.

Is this a normal reaction to a man I'm supposed to dislike? Or is it simply that he's a risky option and it makes the temptation sweeter?

I wish I could tamp down this attraction to him. I hate myself for falling so easily under his charms. I'm not even sure it's charm he gives off.

He's gruff. Direct. Filthy-mouthed and domineering.

And I go weak every single time he goes all alpha on me. It brings me right back to that night in the Vegas hotel room. and me, the easy way he took control over me, thereby allowing me to cede my own carefully constructed control and simply feel.

Do I wish I could throw caution to the wind and let it happen again, give into him one more time without any hesitation? Hell, yes.

But I can't. If I ever allowed it to go there and it was exposed, it could create a big scandal in my office. How would it look? The young, new, *female* owner hooking up with the sexy hockey player she just signed for another year.

It would be a stupid mistake and I'd be a laughing stock among my cohorts in the business.

It's hard enough to keep my head above water in a field dominated by men, especially older rich men who take every opportunity to be condescending and judgmental. I'm a fool if I let Ballas into my bed and into my private life, no matter how much I want to.

A desperate fool who still craves a repeat of that kiss from weeks ago.

It was the most passionate, demanding kiss I've ever had. The mere thought of it has my heart racing and my face flushing as I walk down the corridor toward the bathrooms.

When I left the table, Ballas was heading for the bar in search of another drink. But now as I round the corner into the lounge hallway, I see him walk out of the men's restroom, adjusting his cufflinks.

His dark, charcoal-gray eyes smolder the moment they find mine. And then his gaze drops to my feet and does a slow, appreciative sweep up. The desire in his eyes stops me in my tracks as an intimate smile spreads across his kissable mouth.

An energy sizzles and heats between us and it rages inside me.

"Ballas," I offer cordially, hoping to skirt around him to the ladies' room and thus avoid touching him or brushing against him.

He bows his head like I'm a queen in his presence.

"Karis." The gruffness in his voice is deep and powerful, sending a surge of heat to my belly.

I half-expect him to stop me as I move past, but he doesn't. He lets me by without so much as a sexy, lingering glance.

I use the facilities and spend a few precious minutes checking over my appearance in the mirror. I can see what Daria saw in my face. I do look pale and the dark circles under my eyes are the evidence of just how much I've been pushing myself these past months.

Will this get any easier?

It's so damn hard doing it alone.

Through the doors I can hear the band starting up to move into the dance portion of the event. Ugh. The last thing I want to do is dance with old men who are widowed and looking for a younger wife or so uncoordinated that my poor toes will take a beating by the end of the night.

Or I could call it a night. I consider calling my driver to take me home early. The bags under my eyes certainly think that's a good idea. But the ache in my soul that longs for fun and someone to celebrate my birthday with wants something else entirely.

I apply another dab of red lipstick to my lips and smack them together in a practiced method before stuffing the tube into my clutch. I open the door and step out, my eyes adjusting to the subdued light in the hallway, the sound of the music growing louder in the ears.

The moment I look up, I see Ballas leaning a shoulder casually against the wall, one long leg swung over the other. Is he waiting for me?

I tuck my purse under my arm and walk forward, keeping my gaze in front of me and trying to ignore the immediate pull of lust centering in my belly. He remains still, unmoving from his position, but from my peripheral, I can tell he's watching me. With each step closer, the uncertainty swirls in my head as to the reason I should stay away from him. Doubt creeps into my thoughts, and his confident position has my pulse spinning wildly.

He looks ready to pounce, a beast lying in wait for its prey.

"What are you doing out here?" I ask. The confidence I typically carry is gone, replaced with a string of contradictory emotions about how I feel about this man.

Ballas chuckles low and sensual and my body screams for him. "Well, besides trying to hide from that woman who has been hounding me to dance, I didn't want to leave before I wished you a happy birthday." He straightens to his full

height as I move one step closer. "Do you have plans to celebrate after this?"

A laugh bursts from my lungs. "Nope, no birthday plans.
But thanks for the birthday wishes."

"A fundraiser for your birthday? No birthday bash with your
besties? Or extravagant after-party?"

I shake my head wishing either of those things was true.

"Nothing…" My voice sounds small and shy. "I'm just going to
go home to bed. I'm not big on celebrating birthdays anyway."

Ballas reaches out for my hand, slipping his large, callused
fingers through mine to tug me toward him. My first instinct
is to scan the hallway for anyone who might see this. Ballas's
palm prevents that when he cups my face and redirects my
gaze to his. My secondary reaction is to resist because that's
what I'm good at.

"Ballas…" It's supposed to be a warning but falls flat as I try
to turn in the opposite direction. But his words stop me.

"I want to give you a birthday gift."

"A gift?" I ask, puzzlement wrinkling in my brows.

"Yeah. Every beautiful woman deserves a gift on her
birthday."

He just learned it was my birthday tonight, so how would he
have time to get me a gift? Wait a minute…is he going to
offer to sleep with me? Is sex the gift he has in mind for me?

He can obviously read my thoughts from my confused
expression and he clucks his tongue.

"Get your mind out of the gutter," he jokes darkly, lifting a brow, slipping a hand in his suit pocket. "That'd be low even by my standards. This is what I want to give to you."

Ballas pulls a small, white object out of his suit jacket and holds it out in the palm of his hand. I gingerly pick it up between two fingers and examine the paper napkin origami creation.

"A swan?" A smile comes unbidden to my lips. My cheeks heat. "Where did you get it?"

"I made it for you." Ballas shrugs. "A swan symbolizes grace, beauty, and transformation."

"Oh," I say flatly. I'm a bit floored by the gift's meaning. "Wow. That's beautiful. Thank you."

"There is, of course, still the matter of payback."

My gaze snaps up from the swan to Ballas's face. He rubs a hand over his bearded chin, as if challenging me to object.

Instead of doing the sensible thing and moving away from him, I poke the bear.

The risk is too great and the stakes are too high, but that doesn't to stop me.

I want to know. No...I *need* to know.

"What kind of payback?"

My voice doesn't even sound like my own. It's shaky and thin with a note of anticipation.

He moves so fast I don't have time to voice out even a squeak as suddenly I'm spun around and my back is flush to the wall. Ballas throws his palms above my head and hovers over me, elbows bracketing at my shoulders.

"I think you know exactly what kind of payback, sweetheart."

For all intents and purposes, I should be enraged at the endearment. As if I'm one of his nameless women he's seduced.

Instead, my spine turns to jelly. My body slumps languidly against the wall, clearly affected by his nearness. If it wasn't for the arm that he sweeps around my waist to hold me up, I'd be a puddle on the floor.

Ballas makes no move to encroach any further into my space, but I sense the physical strength that he uses to hold himself back, a departure from his natural instinct to devour me. His masculine scent of spicy amber and bourbon surround me, tickling my senses, and I feel dizzy in his presence. Maybe the champagne is partially to blame, but I might as well be floating off the ground for how light I feel right now.

"Payback or not, it can't happen."

I place my palm on his chest with the intent of pushing him away, but I'm met with hard steel. I need breathing room and a moment to think clearly. When Ballas is this close, my brain goes haywire and my thoughts get fuzzy. His proximity has my body lighting up in a chaotic chorus, loud and buzzing.

"But do you want it to happen?" His voice, deep and sensual, sends a ripple of awareness through my limbs and between my legs.

Oh, how that question leaves me breathless and unable to form a logical response. Do I want him? Do I want what he's offering me? Do I want to take the risk?

The answer is...yes.

Yes.

Yes.

The sound of someone humming a tune grows closer and interrupts my response. I peek under Ballas's arm to see a man round the corner of the hallway. Ballas shifts his weight, blocking me from view. He leans down, his mouth closing in on mine, hovering just inches from my lips, daring me to move in and press against his.

This man is so protective. Considerate. Carnal. Dirty.

Goddamn sexy.

Whoever it is that walks by pays us no mind as he enters the men's bathroom. The door swings open and shut with a soft *whoosh* and we're once again alone together.

Ballas remains still, but he rolls his hand down the curve of my back, and it comes to rest at the base of my spine. With a quick snap of his wrist, he jerks my body into his so I can feel the press of his erection against my belly. His gaze travels over my face and he searches my eyes for an answer to the question.

Someone just cranked up the heat in this place because it's hotter than a furnace room in the basement of the arena.

With his mouth next to my ear, the sound of his grumble is deep and feral and sends a shockwave of desire down my spine. Did he just growl?

The sound has me clenching my legs together to ward off the gravitational pull of his body to mine.

"I asked you a question," he murmurs, the scent of his cologne mixed with his commanding voice flooding my panties with my arousal. I feel his lips feather over my cheek. "All I want is one kiss. Right here. Right now. Just one more fucking taste of you."

My lips part on their own accord. My response is ready to spill out of my mouth but the words get stuck in my throat as my body takes over. My arms loop around the back of his neck, hands grasping at the hair hanging low at his nape.

What harm could come of a kiss for my birthday?

"Just one," I say breathlessly, tipping my head back to stare into his dark, stormy-gray eyes. I lick my lips. "One birthday kiss."

He chuckles dryly. "I don't care what you call it, sweetheart, but it's long overdue."

His mouth crashes harshly against mine his demanding and possessive lips covering me with hungry kisses. I've waited for this so long that my reservations have all but disappeared the minute his tongue pushes past my lips and explores the recesses of my mouth as I obediently open for him.

I can hear him murmur, '*good girl*' against my mouth when he frames my face the roughness of his hands and the delicious scrape of his beard over my cheeks a reminder of how they once felt against my inner thighs. His mouth slants to devour more of me, his tongue hard and searching.

I raise on my tiptoes to offer him everything I have and I take pleasure in the groan that escapes his throat. This kiss is frenzied and messy. Every inch of my body is feverish. My nipples pucker against my dress in response to this forbidden desire burning inside me. My heart hammers wildly under my sternum, telling me everything I already knew.

This is not just one simple birthday kiss. It will never *be just one.*

It's lethal in its potency, like a bomb exploding and leveling all in its path.

This kiss breaks my resolve and will ruin me.

13

Ballas

Under normal circumstances, I would break the kiss and encourage her with a cocky line to continue it somewhere more private where I could do wicked things with her and to her, bringing all her sexual fantasies to life.

I'd give Karis a birthday to remember.

With Karis, however, it all comes with a mountain of complexity.

Not surprisingly, she's the first to come to her senses and pull away.

"Ballas, I can't...I won't sleep with you tonight," she tells me in a breathless voice.

The last word, however, comes out as a potential loophole and invitation. Smiling smugly, I raise my hand to her face and gently rub her swollen bottom lip with my thumb.

"Okay, not tonight...maybe tomorrow then?"

A smile breaks free and she tuts, gently shoving at my breastbone. I chuckle and back away, crooking my elbow so she can hook a hand through it as I lead her back to the ballroom.

Before we get to the doors, she stops and checks the time. "I should probably call it a night. Tomorrow's the first game, after all. You ready for it?"

"Sweetheart, I'm *always* ready for it."

IN THE END, I saw Karis out to her waiting car and then returned to my condo alone, still horny as hell but with a satisfied smile.

It probably saved my sorry ass in the end since we have our first preseason home game tonight. When I was in my twenties, I could fuck all night before a game the next day and kill it on the ice without so much as an ache or pain.

Now it would likely kick me in the ass. I'm just happy it's preseason and I have some breathing room before things get serious.

The morning practice wasn't too bad but damn my joints are screaming for some WD-40. The best I can do is get in the ice tub for three minutes and then hop on the massage for a rubdown to keep my muscles loose for tonight.

"How was the rest of the gala last night, Keeners? You go home with some lucky lady?"

I glance over my shoulder to see Canners through the open doorway of the equipment room where he's taping up his stick and waiting for his blades to be sharpened. I give him a long, hard appraisal, wondering if he suspects anything between Karis and me. I did my best not to be overtly flirtatious with her at the dinner table, but it still felt glaringly obvious how we are together.

There's nothing in his expression to think he noticed anything, I reluctantly submerge into the icy bath and shake my head, lips trembling from the cold. "No. But thanks a lot for leaving me high and dry, eh? I got stuck dancing with the woman who was the highest bidder on our auction item. I swear she thought I came with the package as her personal boy toy for the night."

Canners laughs. "Sorry 'bout that, bro, but the wife and I had some *things* to take care of before relieving the babysitter."

I quirk an eyebrow. "I didn't realize that hotel had pay-by-the-hour room rates."

A roll of tape comes sailing at my head and I duck so it misses me and lands on the tile floor.

"Just you wait, Keeners. Someday you'll have kids who will eat into all the precious time you have with the woman you love. You gotta find the time when you can and get creative or lose it."

I reach for the towel hanging over the edge of the bath and step out of the tub, my body racked with shivers, my balls frozen and shriveled against my legs.

The same type of pain I experienced with the blue balls I had last night. If that's what Cannfield deals with on the reg because of a baby cockblocking him and his wife, I will easily say *no thank you* to any future kids. Fortunately, my brother has produced grandchildren for my parents, so there's no need for me to carry on the Keeney family name.

I bend over and pick up the roll of tape from the wet puddle on the floor and hand it back to Brett.

"Sorry, not sorry. I'm good with my lifestyle. You chose kids."

The massage therapist, Kip, finishes up with Soren, who, based on the sounds of moaning, is practically orgasming on the table during his massage.

"You giving him a handy over there, Kip?" I quip, tugging my towel tighter around my waist.

Soren growls his usual bad-tempered response, flipping me off as he throws his legs over the table. With hands knuckling the edge to stabilize himself, his eyes are half-lidded and his hair a messy stack of blond strands, his head droops forward. Yeah, he definitely enjoyed the massage work, orgasm or not.

I slap our new Austrian goalie's shoulder. "Tough night last night, Wolf?"

He grumbles something in German and gingerly places his feet on the ground while Kip starts to change the sheets on the table.

"Nah, I'm good," he says, the word good sounding like *goot*. "I'm ready for tonight. You?"

"Fuck yeah, I am. Who knows, it could be my last opener." It rolls off my tongue like it's no biggie, but the very thought of it hits like a punch to the gut.

Wolf grunts and Kip slaps the table as an indicator for me to hop on. I do as he says, gripping the towel to keep it wrapped around my hips as I stretch out prone to lie on my belly. Then I place my head in the face cradle and groan with fatigue.

"None of us know the future, but I'm glad I get to play with you, Keeney." Soren smacks me on the back. "And not against you."

He chuckles and walks off to the showers, his bare ass in full view as he goes. Soren may be a grumpy loner who doesn't care if his parts on display, but he's a fucking good goalie and I'm happy he's with us this year.

With Kip's strong precise hands, I soon understand why Wolf was in such complete bliss. My body needed this.

Almost as much as it needed Karis.

Bummer I'm only getting massage relief from Kip and not the sexual release I'd wanted with Karis last night.

The thought of marching upstairs to Karis's office and blinding her with a kiss, followed by fucking her up against those glass windows like I did in Vegas, has my cock twitching for relief.

And laying out on a massage therapist's table is not a great place to have a hard on.

I refocus my thoughts on the game ahead. It may only be

preseason but it's against one of our toughest competitors and now the team of my archnemesis, Sergei Russo.

Russo was traded from Dallas to Toronto at the end of last season. I may have the nickname of The Beast, but it's Russo who is the biggest brute of them all. He's always been a dirty player and ends up in the sin bin more times in a game than the rest of his team combined.

He plays dirty and rough and nobody likes him—not even his own teammates. I suppose that's why Toronto wanted him. Their win record last year sucked so they're probably trying to shake up their lines and need a guy who is going to do just that.

My entire career I've skated against the biggest and strongest players, guys who have one goal in mind, and that's to light the lamp. To do that, we blueliners have to block and attack to guard our net and the puck. It's a full-on physical contact sport.

I've been checked against the boards, cross-checked from behind and concussed many times. I'm a hockey player—I get hit—but Russo's hits are next-level hard.

Whereas other competitors are looking to win, Russo's veins are literally filled with ice. He's always out for blood. If he hasn't bloodied someone up before the end of the game, he hasn't succeeded.

In this league, I fear no one. Except Russo. His play scares the shit out of me. I shiver now just thinking about the game tonight, and Kip takes my reaction as a sign he's found a spot.

"You okay?" He presses a knot in my glutes and I groan, taking a page out of Soren's book.

"Yeah, right there."

And he begins to work me over, putting me in a deep trance for the next fifteen minutes.

I haven't slept this soundly in ages.

14

———

K aris

I couldn't sleep last night for a myriad of reasons.

Okay, fine. It was one reason and one reason only. One huge reason with wide shoulders, dark eyes and kisses that turn me into a babbly mess.

Ballas Keeney.

The man has occupied my thoughts for weeks and now has me so keyed up since last night's kiss that I can't think straight.

I'm more than a little frazzled as a I pace my office floor, biting my nails as I listen to Charlie, the Pilot's media relations manager, and Marek tell me something I'd hoped I'd never hear.

Charlie is filling us in on Hammond Greis, a small forward on the team, who was just arrested on charges of battery and assault against his girlfriend and the mother of his child.

My heart aches for the woman and her child, and my anger spikes to an all-time high as I listen to Marek and Charlie's report on what Greis did. Allegedly did, that is.

Thankfully, there is time to hash out plans and figure out the best way to handle this since the NBA season won't begin for another six weeks. I'm happy to hear that my staff is on the same page as me and we'll be taking swift action to handle and the repercussions against Hammond.

Even when things are going smoothly, the problem with being an active owner of two teams in two very different leagues is that it's exhausting and the business is never-ending. Up until now, I think I've handled it all pretty well, even when I'm being pulled in two directions. I've effectively balanced the time requirements for both teams, as well as the personal obligations related to managing my uncle's care, even if it means I have no personal life to speak of.

The other unfortunate problem is that I have zero band-width to deal with these unexpected curve balls that get thrown my way. It has me wanting to eat a jumbo-sized bag of Skittles while burying my head in the sand.

"Has the team ever encountered something like this in the past?" I ask, continuing to pick at my nail between my teeth as I wear a tread over my carpet. "What protocols are in place? Since it's in the hands of the law, do we need to speak to the commissioner?"

My morning started out like a dream because I was still floating in a dream-like state from last night's kiss that left me blissed out from the moment Ballas closed the door to my car and sent me home.

I replayed that kiss all night while I lay awake in a state of sexual awareness, still tingling from the timbre of his low voice and the promise it held. My body yearned for the feel of his warm hands as they cupped my jaw, and the smooth glide and sensual heat of his tongue. I was lost in wanting more of the rough texture of his scruff as they scraped over my lips and over my sensitive skin.

The entire memory had my body prickling with heat until I could no longer stand it. While still in my bed, I slid my hand beneath the sheet and between my thighs, fingers slipping through my wetness as I imagined Ballas's fingers easing in and out of me instead of my own. I was so wet and turned on it took me less than twenty seconds to push myself to orgasm.

I'd hoped the solo session would have carried me forward through both my work day and tonight's game against Toronto.

Instead of an easy morning, I listen to Marek and Charlie discuss Hammond's case while I make a note to conduct a careful review of the Vikings internal policies as well as read over the rules the NHL has laid out. As I look down at the hand holding the pen, I realize I've bitten my nails to the quick.

As Charlie finishes his report, Marek adds his insight into this horrible situation. "The Pilots haven't had any problems of this nature that I'm aware of since I've been here, but there have been players in the league in recent years who have been arrested on domestic violence charges. The league commissioner determines the punishment, in accordance with the Players Association."

Charlie jumps in. "Which usually consists of suspending the player a minimum of 10 games."

"Ten games? That's ridiculous," I scoff, frustrated over such leniency. Although it wasn't against anyone in the league, domestic violence should never be tolerated amongst players.

"Yes, I agree with you Karis, but it's the NBA Players Association and their policies under the collective bargaining agreement that protect the players' contractual interest and their future roles on the teams. If it's any consolation though, the legal system won't care about any of that. If the player is found guilty or convicted of a felony, it won't matter that they are represented by a contract."

"Physically harming a woman or a child is reprehensible. The team, and the league, should have a zero-tolerance policy. Period. End of story."

My declaration is marked with a brief silence from the other end of the line.

Marek speaks first. "Charlie and I have been in this league a long time. We've seen the stance on domestic violence and assaults change quite dramatically, thank God. But remember, Karis, no matter how much we want to implement that type of policy, we can't contradict the league. We can only impose the fines and suspended time as dictated."

I fist my hands to prevent myself from picking up my candy jar and throwing it at the wall in anger. How can I, a female owner of a professional men's basketball team, pretend this is all okay in public? And how can I use this as a preventative war cry for changes to the existing policies on the Vikings team?

What would Marv do?

I finally sit down but get more and more agitated as the call goes on, finally my elbows on top of my desk to hang my head in my hands. I want to scream and shout over the absurdity of these rules, but instead I take a deep breath instead and let it out slowly. With each passing second, I come to my own conclusions.

Fuck whatever else has been done in the past.

I will not condone this behavior on either of my teams.

"Marek, I want you to contact the NBA commissioner and set up a meeting for us to discuss this. I want to make it abundantly clear that we will not tolerate violent acts from our players and expect their support on that. And Charlie, you'll put out our statement in the press of the same nature, but with one caveat."

"What's that?" Charlie asks. I can practically see him twirling the ends of his burnt-orange mustache, his oddly cute trademark facial hair.

"That I, Karis Spurlock, will be drawing a line in the sand, and will be going to battle for what is right. The time for the league to adopt a zero-tolerance policy is now and I'm going to spearhead that initiative."

Oh shit. I may have just bit off more than I can chew.

WHILE MOST OF the players have gone home for their pre-game rituals, I do some research into the NHL's history on handling sexual assault and domestic violence cases amongst its players. No one disputes that hockey is a violent sport, that's easy to see. The problem that seems to exist is how that violence and toxic masculinity bleeds over off the ice and into personal lives.

Based on my quick scan of articles written on the subject, the NHL has far less incidents of allegations of domestic violence than any other sport and the league has taken swift action against the few players who have been arrested for such matters, not leaving it up to just the individual teams to make the decision. The teams conduct their own internal investigation, and if they find the player has engaged in conduct that is unacceptable or that violates the terms and policies, they can suspend players indefinitely without pay and then put them on unconditional waivers.

Now that's what I'm talking about. Good job, boys.

Do the right thing and stand on principle.

I'm all for due process, but players need to know there are consequences to their actions outside the ice rink or the hard woods. They represent the team and live their lives in the public eye; therefore it must be beyond reproach. I don't think that's a lot to ask for guys who are paid millions.

My mind races with all the information I obtained during my thirty-minute research session, as I now lay on the massage table that's been set up in my office, on the receiving end of a massage from the team's therapist, Kip. Christine had thought it would be a good idea and called it her birthday gift to me ahead of tonight's big game.

"These shoulders of yours are tighter than the muscles on some of the players I worked on this morning," he jokes, digging his thumbs and fingers into the soft tissue of my upper body. "I think you should go see my friend, Somer. She owns a yoga and meditation studio. She's fantastic and I bet she would be a great help in learning how to manage your stress levels."

I make a laughing sound that comes out as a cough. "What gives you the impression that I'm stressed?"

"You mean, besides these boulders?" he teases, massaging my scapula area with more pressure to indicate said boulders. "Everyone has stress in their lives, Karis, but each of us responds differently. You obviously hold it all up here."

I moan when he rolls his thumbs into the tissue at the base of my neck.

"On top of which, you still have residual scar tissue, and that must be very painful."

"It is," I agree softly. He doesn't ask me any questions about my scar except if it's too painful in areas and whether he should avoid those spots.

He continues to manipulate the connective tissue and ligaments as I finally begin to let go and relax.

"Everyone notices just how hard you work, Karis. You have a reputation of being—"

"An ice queen. Yes, I've heard."

Kip's hands leave my body momentarily and I hear the sound of a bottle being pumped. His warm palms, now slick again with lotion, return to my back and continue to knead the sore muscles along my spine.

"A workaholic is what I was going to say. I'm sure it hasn't been easy to step into Marvin's shoes. But in just the few months you've been here, you've done a lot of great things. Honestly, it's rather nice to have a woman's leadership woven through the organization," he offers, his compliment hitting me straight in the feelers.

Tears suddenly well up in my eyes, working to spring free. I swallow down the emotions swirling inside me, knowing it's just a physical byproduct of the release the massage provides.

"Thank you, Kip. That's really nice of you to say."

Kip has me flip over onto my back facing up, kindly turning away as I maneuver myself under the sheet. I stretch my legs out in front of me and settle on my back. He adjusts the pillow under my neck and leans down to whisper in my ear.

"And excuse me for saying so but fuck anyone who labels you or calls you names that aren't accurate. They're just jealous old men."

I snort with laughter. "Yeah, well. I guess working hard and doing what's expected of me naturally equates to being a badass bitch in some people's eyes."

"That's right. But you're *our* badass bitch and don't you forget it."

Kip continues to work on me for a few more minutes as I consider where things are at with the team and our potential success in the year ahead.

Considering that Kip works closely with the crew inside these locker room walls, I ask him about the game tonight.

"What are your thoughts on the team's chances tonight against Toronto?"

This apparently opens the flood gates for Kip, who is quick to give me his unfiltered opinion.

"I think we look like an experienced team with some really strong players. From what I saw during training camp this week, they've gelled well together," he offers, fingers digging into my neck and sending me to heaven. "All the lines look ready to go."

Then his tone quiets as concern threads through his voice. "But I will admit, I'm a little worried about the Sergei and Ballas matchup tonight."

My limber muscles suddenly cramp and stiffen at the remark and the mention of Ballas's name. I prod him on for more information. I've heard Sergei Russo mentioned in passing and on the sports broadcasts as being a tough player, but I'm not familiar with any inside information.

"What do you mean?" Ballas is a strong player and whoever this Russo is, he must have played against him in the past.

Kip moves down my body, removing the sheet from each leg as he begins working on my thighs and calves. I let out a groan. I can't imagine how the players work through their pain.

"No one knows what's behind the feud, but it goes back a long time. Sergei is known for his hard-hitting tactics on good days, but he always seems out for Ballas's blood, like it's personal."

"Hmm." I contemplate this backstory and wonder what the beef could be about. I don't know Sergei except that he was on the trade reports this summer. No one has ever mentioned anything to me. "Well, I'm sure the Beast can handle his own against a player like that."

I say this to protect myself, to force myself not to care about Ballas's on-ice conflict with another player.

There's already a shit ton of things on my plate right now and in my emotional bucket is overflowing. I don't have room to worry about Ballas. He's a big boy, he can handle himself.

Ballas Keeney is already occupying more than enough space in my head. I don't need to give him any more real estate.

15

B allas

There's probably a million and one reasons Russo hates me.

Maybe it's because I'm a seven-time NHL All-Star and he's not. Or that I've won the Norris trophy in my fifth year and he's never come close. Or because I've won the Stanley Cup in my career and he's never been on a winning team.

Or none of those reasons could matter to him and it's simply because I witnessed something he did years ago and he wants to make sure I never mention it.

Whatever the case, Russo is the only guy I've ever truly despised and tonight I get a dose of his shit.

Thankfully, in the first five minutes of the first period, my team sets the record straight with three back-to-back goals, two of which I was awarded assists. One was to Costa and another to Ax, easily shutting down Sergei's attempt at takeaways.

The flipside to this scoring lead as we take the ice into the second period is that it's sent Sergei into a tailspin. His dark eyes stare me down as we wait for the puck to drop. His glare tells me he wants revenge for making him look bad tonight.

Well, fuck him. He should play better then.

I get into position, keeping my stick light in my gloves, and watch as the puck bounces from the ref's hands and is immediately dished out from Costa over to Ax, who swiftly maneuvers it with the speed and agility he's known for down the right side of the ice.

With Russo on his heels, I skate toward Ax, positioning myself on his left to both block the team and be open for a pass.

I see Costa is in front of me and to the left, and I know he's going to be on the receiving end of the pass.

Ax chips the puck to me on his backhand to me, and Costa is ready and waiting to receive the pass from me.

I dangle it around Sergei, first to his left and then to the right, his stick jamming in front me, looking to gain possession. But I'm too fast for him and I let the puck fly toward Costa, who is now heading toward the net to take his shot.

What occurs next happens in a blur.

As soon as the puck leaves my stick, I skate around toward the right side of the boards, ready to be there for a rebound if Costa's shot misses the net or the puck is deflected. Russo is on my tail. I hear him grunt and smell his desperation.

The next thing I know, he gets a piece of me from behind with a cross-check to the boards.

I don't expect the hit because the puck is out of play.

Russo's hard, dirty hit is lethal and absolutely illegal.

But that apparently doesn't stop him from ramming me again. My head flies forward into the glass and snaps back like a bobblehead doll.

The next thing I know, I'm laid out face down on the ice. The world spins in a hazy pain, and my head swirls like an amusement park ride.

There's buzzing in my ears. Or is that the crowd booing Russo?

I slowly try to rise, to make my way up to my knees, but my arms and legs give out from under me and I'm flat again, my body involuntarily collapsing back to the ice. My vision goes in and out, growing dimmer as I notice two pairs of skates at my side.

"You okay, Keeners?"

I blink. I can't move my head or look up at Costa

Then I feel a hand on my back. Our trainer, David, is at my side.

"Tell me your name."

I want to laugh because it's a stupid question. Who the fuck wouldn't know their name? But the question gives me pause.

My name? That's easy...it's...

Fuuuuck.

"Can you stand?" A hand wraps around my elbow and he brings me to my feet.

"I'm fine." I try to push him away. but the wobble in my stance clearly tells a different story. I'm good and truly fucked.

David scowls. "That's what I thought. We're getting you off the ice, Ballas."

I grumble but I know he's only doing his job. It's mandatory that I get evaluated after a hit like that.

"You were motionless and couldn't get up on your own," Costa tells me as he and David hold onto my elbows and start heading to the bench. "Fuckin' Russo really got ya, man. Motherfucker."

The cheering of our fans fills the arena as I sit down, but all of it's muffled for me.

It's impossible not have had concussions when you've played hockey as long as I have. It's the nature of this violent sport. The helmets do little against the hard impact of ice, boards, or other bodies.

The fact that this is probably my fourth or fifth injury does not bode well for me starting this season. If it's assessed as a concussion, I won't even be able to start in our first regular season games. The league over the years has also implemented policies for concussion protocol. Guidelines to evaluate and treat head injuries during play.

"We'll take care of Russo. You hear me, Keeners?"

That's the thing about teammates. They always have your

back. I have no doubt there will be some gloves off in the third period on my behalf.

And when I'm fully recovered—whenever that may be—there will come a time when I provide my own payback to Sergei Russo.

Mark my words. It will happen.

I'M USHERED into the medical exam area next to our team's locker where the lights are too bright and they give me a headache.

Dr. Stanley, the team physician, and David poke and prod, and ask me a fuck ton of questions while examining me on the table.

"I'm sure you know the drill," begins Dr. Stanley, an older gentleman with graying hair at the temples, with a soft-spoken voice and kind smile. "But we'll need to conduct a full acute assessment, starting with our SCAT5 test."

I'm familiar with this testing app that is part of the NHL concussion protocol and it's been used on me in the past. It's the physician's way of identifying and diagnosing the severity of my concussion and provide the baseline testing and analysis of my cognitive function. In a nutshell, whether my brain is messed up.

As the first round of tests begin, the door of the medical room bursts open and my head lolls in that direction, where I see an angel walking toward me.

Only not just any angel.

Karis.

"Jesus Christ, is Ballas okay?"

Her voice comes out in a panicked rush as she scurries over to the side of the table where I'm propped up with the doctor in front of me. Most of my gear was at some point removed and I'm left in my long-sleeved compression shirt and my jock shorts.

The menthol smell from muscle lotions and the stench of sweat are barely noticeable as I'm surrounded by Karis's fresh floral scent.

I close my eyes, which is a big mistake, and my body sways to the side and into the arms of this beautiful woman.

"You worried about me, sweetheart?" The corners of my mouth tip up into a lopsided grin. I'm acting like a sloppy drunk. I feel like one, too.

As if my words just bit her like a venomous snake, she stumbles backwards so suddenly that David has to grab my shoulder to keep me from falling off the table.

All eyes are pinned on me, Karis's blown wide.

It's then that I realize exactly how I just addressed our team's owner.

Oops. My bad.

David snorts at the comment, treating it like a joke.

"He must be concussed. He'll probably call me babe next, eh?"

I would laugh, except nausea swirls in my belly and my mouth begins to flood with saliva. I gag and try to tamp down the sickness climbing up my throat. Karis steps back, picks up a nearby trashcan at the head of the table, and shoves it in front of me just as I hunch forward and vomit. Unfortunately, I didn't make it in time and I think Karis's shoes got the brunt of it.

After emptying the contents of my stomach a second time, David removes the trashcan from Karis's hands and I promptly fall back onto the pillow.

I close my eyes and smile. "Thanks, babe."

And then I pass out.

16

———

K aris

When will this day be over?

It started out with a vivid sex dream about Ballas and then rapidly went downhill from there with Ballas's vomit all over my shoes when he missed the bucket.

When I saw Ballas hit the boards and collapse from my position in the owner's box, I knew it was bad. Like, really, *really* bad.

All the anxiety I've bottled up from dealing with my uncle's condition all these months came rushing back in an avalanche of PTSD. I barely waited around long enough to hear the official's call against Sergei Russo before I ran down here to the locker room where I now wait for the doctor to evaluate Ballas.

The ref ruled it a major penalty. The crowd was not happy and expressed their opinions with loud booing and jeers against both the ref and Russo who should've been booted out of the rest of the game for misconduct.

David thoughtfully brings me a washcloth to clean up my soiled suit jacket and shoes, while the doctor continues his evaluation of Ballas.

"How long does it normally take to assess a concussion?" I ask as David and I move outside the closed-door room to offer Ballas privacy. I take a seat on the bench so I can slip off my heels and wipe them clean.

David shrugs, folding his arms in front of his chest. His lips purse in a slight frown.

"It really depends on the person. There are a ton of questions on the cognitive screening related to concentration. There's a neurological screen, immediate memory recall, a balance and mobility check—here, let me show you."

David pulls up his phone, typing in some keys to bring up an app. He sits down next to me and offers me a view of his screen.

"It's called the SCAT5. Short for Sport Concussion Assessment Tool. The 5 is for the fifth version of it."

I watch as he scrolls through the various components of the test.

"It's all very standardized and used in all sports nowadays. Even peewee football."

I look up through the window into the medical room, the curtains left open so we can see Ballas sitting on the edge of the exam table, his brow wrinkled in concentration. He's shaking his head in disgust.

David huffs out a resigned sigh. "This isn't Ballas's first bad hit. He was out for three games last season for a similar issue. But not like the hit he took tonight. Damn, that was nasty."

"The officials only ruled it a major penalty," I grouse, still angry over that slight. "Russo should've received more than that for that dirty hit."

It seems that Kip was right about what he said earlier about Russo. That man either has it out for Ballas specifically or is just a batshit-crazy dirty player. I've never witnessed anything quite like that hit. My job now is to voice my opinion loudly over Russo's unsportsmanlike tactics and to ensure he is properly and justly punished for such behavior.

But for now, I need to know that Ballas will be okay.

Ballas's slip-of-the-tongue earlier in front of everyone is certainly cause for concern of his current mental state of confusion. Otherwise, he wouldn't have used that term of endearment for me except in private, which he has done on occasion.

I can't say I wasn't amused when Ballas called me sweetheart in front of two of the team's staff, but I was also slightly embarrassed. I'm sure my face flushed beet red when I jumped away from Ballas the way I did.

If anyone even caught a whiff of inappropriate conduct between Ballas and me, even if it was in the past, it would be reputation-damaging for me and surely diminish any of the respect I've worked so hard to gain.

I'm sure there's an unwritten rule that a team owner shouldn't fuck their players.

I would be a mockery of my colleagues in the NHL ownership group if it were ever found out that I've slept with Ballas.

Which is why each time we've kissed, I've told Ballas it can't happen again.

Fat lot of good that's done me since I've allowed it to happen. *Twice.*

What can I say? I'm a glutton for punishment and he's a friggin' great kisser.

But why does he keep on trying? Ballas can get any woman he wants. There are plenty of women eager to fuck a hockey player without strings attached.

He was clear the night we hooked up that he's a one-and-done kind of guy and would remain a confirmed bachelor during the course of his career.

What's changed? Does he just like the challenge? Is it the secret conquest that turns him on? Or does he just like the rejection?

None of that matters right now anyway and takes a backseat to his injury. After thirty minutes, Dr. Stanley finally opens the door and invites us to join the inside.

David gestures for me to enter first. I walk in to find Ballas's head hanging low, his legs dangling over the edge of the table.

The doctor begins, his tone serious and firm. "Ballas, my initial assessment isn't looking great. Your medical chart indicates you've been concussed numerous times in the past five years, which only compounds the severity level with each subsequent hit. You failed your recall and retention tests and have demonstrated several of the red flags on the assessment. My medical advice is for you to rest five-to-seven days and after each 24-hour period, if there's any regression, add another day before you play again."

"Fuck!" Ballas shouts angrily, slapping a palm down against the table. Loud enough and with enough vitriol behind it to shake my core.

I instinctively place my hand on his shoulder, uncertain whether it's to calm him or comfort me.

"If it were up to me, I'd strongly recommend you consider an earlier-than-planned retirement. More hits like this could be dangerous to your future neurological function."

The doctor makes notes in his tablet as the oxygen is sucked out of the room, making it nearly impossible to breathe.

"Dr. Stanley," I interject. I have very little familiarity of the concussion follow-up. "What should we do now? I mean, what should Ballas's care include?"

The doctor clears his throat and removes his latex gloves.

"A lot can change in the span of a few hours with concussions. Ballas will need someone to be with him over the next twenty-four hours, which is a very critical period, and continued monitoring and evaluation after that for quite a while..."

My gaze snaps to Ballas, who is still pale but has more color than the gray pallor he wore when I first walked in.

"Do you have someone who can care for you, Ballas?" I don't even know if he has family close by. The idea that he might have a girlfriend or a friends-with-benefits he would call on makes my stomach roll considering the proposition he made to me just last night after the fundraiser dinner.

If I find out he's a cheater…

"I'll be fine on my own. Never had a problem before."

Dr. Stanley's eyes meet mine over Ballas's head and he gives a disapproving head shake.

"You will not leave this arena tonight without a chaperone to escort you," he promises sternly, making notes on a chart. "And you need to refrain from any physical or cognitive demands for the next forty-eight hours. No driving, no alcohol or other substances…"

Ballas's voice is weak but his response is provacative. "Does that include sex?"

I eyeball him but he just shrugs a shoulder and then winces in pain.

"Looks like you just answered your own question," I retort and look at the physician, who is doing his best to keep a straight face. "I'll make sure Ballas has someone to watch over him for the next two nights."

With that, the doctor prints out several pages of the symptoms to watch out for that could put Ballas in harm's way if not treated immediately.

As Dr. Stanley and David leave the room, we hear the final buzzer ringing through the open door, noting the end of the game. Ballas gingerly lifts his gaze to mine, quirking an eyebrow.

"Just who exactly are you assigning to my bedside tonight?"

Without missing a beat and without so much as a quiver in my voice, I reply, "Me."

17

B allas

"Remind me again why I'm here instead of at my place?"

My question echoes through the foyer as we enter Karis's penthouse condo. The condo, she explained in the car on the way over, belongs to her uncle Marvin. She's just living in it temporarily while she's handling business in Vancouver. Karis didn't want to buy anything for herself given the fact that she still hopes he'll recover and return to Vancouver soon.

In the meantime, he's receiving twenty-four-hour care at his mansion down in Seattle.

"Because it's easier on me," she says matter-of-factly, hanging her purse on a hook and removing her shoes to place them on a mat on the floor. She sets my overnight bag down, which she refused to let me carry after we'd packed it up at my condo and pins me with a stare. "I have my office set up here so I can work while you sleep. I also am confident that my guestroom is clean. Yours might be suspect."

I try not to snort and scan around the elegantly decorated apartment that was just a short ten-minute drive from the arena. Although I'd have preferred to be in my own bed tonight, I can't exactly complain with the way Karis jumped in and offered to help me out in my time of need.

How crazy would I have to be to say no to my beautiful boss who invited me to stay at her condo for the next two nights?

My gaze finds the wall-to-wall windows overlooking the city of Vancouver below. I'm acutely reminded of the night we spent together in Vegas, when I fucked her up against the windows high above the Strip. There's also a giant pool table in the back of the room. That doesn't help in tamping down my desire when now all I can imagine is laying her naked body across the table and sliding into the pocket.

I shoot her an innocent look.

"You mean, I won't be sleeping with you?" I pause and lift a suggestive brow. "What if I need something in the middle of the night?"

Karis whips her head toward me, her jaw drops incredulously. "Ballas, this isn't...I wasn't...you're not sleeping with me!"

Her panicked expression and high-pitched voice are priceless. A laugh I've been holding back bursts from my chest. I may have a head injury but I can still have some flirtatious fun with Karis.

"Oh, princess. You should see your face right now."

An angry little scowl purses at her lips and she grumbles, lifting my gym bag in her hand before stomping off down a hallway. "Not funny, Ballas. Now take off your shoes and follow me."

"I can take off my clothes, too."

She flattens me with a glare and I chuckle, wisely following her orders with no further commentary, and pad down the hallway after her. My eyes sweep in an appreciative gaze over the feminine curves of her hips and ass, which sway in a sexy saunter. She may be wearing a demure pantsuit befitting a wealthy businesswoman, but goddamn if she isn't a fucking knockout.

My brain may feel muzzy at the moment but that doesn't stop my fingers from itching with the memories of roaming every inch of her spectacular body. From behind my zipper, my cock begs to do it again.

Shit, this is not how I imagined ending up at Karis's home for the night. Now both my dick and my head throb with not a damn thing I can do about it. Living under the same roof as Karis for the next twenty-four hours will be painful to remember she is off-limits.

How the hell did I get here with Karis? It was supposed to be a one-night stand, no further complications. Our lives were never supposed to intersect again except through our mutual ties to Marek and Marv.

Yet here we are. Instead of getting less complicated, we continue to be pulled into the same orbit, connected by these strange cosmic circumstances. If you believe in that stuff. Which I don't. But damned if there's any other logical way to explain why I'm still so attracted to this woman.

Karis opens a door at the end of the long hallway and flips on the light to a large, guestroom room. She steps inside and walks over to the bed.

With efficient movements, she leans over and pulls down the plush comforter, removing the decorative pillows propped at the headboard. Then she turns on the bedside lamp and lets out a satisfied breath.

"Why don't you get comfortable and I'll order some food for dinner. Any objections to chicken parm? The Italian eatery at the end of the street is delicious. I'll bring it in when it arrives."

My stomach growls at the suggestion. "Nah, that sounds great. Thanks."

She nods. "Good. And after that it's doctor's orders. Dr. Stanley said you should get plenty of rest so that's what you're going to do."

I chuckle. If there's one thing I've learned tonight about Karis, it's that she is a rule follower to the nth degree. I can only imagine her when she was in school, enthusiastically raising her hand to answer every question the teacher asked the class and diligently completing her homework for extra credit.

So very unlike me, for sure. All I cared about was playing hockey and pushing myself through to the elite levels to ensure I made the NHL.

Jesus, that was so many years and injuries ago.

Karis has taken everything Dr. Stanley said as gospel. With only one exception—allowing me to gather up some extra underwear, socks, and T-shirts when we swung by my apartment after leaving the arena—she's done all the heavy lifting. That's not something I've ever allowed a woman to do for me. Admittedly, it's nice to be taken care of in this way.

Otherwise, she's played everything by the letter and the rules of concussion after care. She even snatched away my phone when I tried to check the latest sports news while in the car, not giving me a chance to read the reports about what had happened.

I still have no recollection of the few minutes leading up to my injury beyond his usual chirping. But everything is blank, so I want to see it play out in the highlights reel, even if it will only make my hatred of Sergei grow stronger.

Karis types away at her phone, presumably ordering the food online, as I pull out clean shorts from my bag and undo my jeans. The snick of the zipper has her head popping up. She blushes as I push them down past my knees.

"Oh, let me give you some privacy," she mutters, quickly averting her eyes and turning her back to me. I snicker and she snaps her gaze back to mine.

"Nothing new to see here. You've seen it all before."

I make quick work and climb into bed as she finishes placing the order. When her eyes drift to me once more, they soften.

"How are you feeling? I'll go find you some Tylenol and water. You'll need to stay hydrated and you'll be due for some in an hour."

Before she leaves, I reach for her wrist and clutch it in my hand.

"Why am I here, Karis?"

Confusion wrinkles her brows. I tug her forward so she's flush with the edge of the bed. So close I smell her sweet, feminine scent and my dick perks up with interest.

"Isn't it obvious?" she says stubbornly, lifting her shoulders like I'm an idiot. "You have a concussion and the doc said you needed someone to take care of you for forty-eight hours and you said you didn't have anyone."

I shake my head, the corners of my mouth tipping into a knowing smirk. "Nah, that's not it. At least not all of it. Try again, princess."

She huffs, her eyes pinning me with a hard stare. Her tone changes back into that bossy one she uses in the workplace. Karis's expression turns edgy and a defensive frown forms across her mouth.

"Stop calling me princess."

"Don't dodge my question, *sweetheart*," I drawl in reply. "Why did you offer to bring me here? Would you have done it for another player?"

She struggles to move within my solid grasp and I relent and reluctantly release her. She takes two steps backwards and folds her arms over her chest. She hesitates, calculating the words she wants to say, and chews on her bottom lip.

"I...probably not. If you must know, I was scared. Okay? Are you happy now?"

I push myself up against the headboard and scoot over, making room on the side of the bed for her to sit down. I pat the spot, silently offering her the invitation. Probably not the wisest choice if I'm trying to keep my distance. What can I say? Concussion brain has me making poor decisions.

She shakes her head in refusal. At least she's thinking straight.

"Why were you scared?" I ask quietly. Some deep part of me wants to hear that she cares about me, feels the same connection I do. There is no denying that the attraction between us has lingered and grown unexpectedly.

My question seems to act like a sledgehammer that has finally broken through the wall Karis has constructed and allows the levee to break.

I watch as her entire body deflates like a balloon and tears flood from her eyes.

It feels all too similar to the night I flew to Seattle when her uncle was admitted to the hospital. When I showed up at that hospital in an uncharacteristically sympathetic decision—God knows why—to comfort her during her time of need.

I stretch my arms out to her and this time she comes willingly. Karis sits on the edge of the bed and curls into my arms. I hold her tightly, her wet tears soaking into my T-shirt.

Have I ever just held a woman in bed without it leading to something sexual? Karis brings something out in me that no one else ever has before.

"Hey, come on now...*shhh*," I murmur, my lips pressed against the top of her head. "I'm fine. Everything's okay, princess."

I stroke her hair as she sniffles softly until her tears have quieted and her body relaxes. When she pushes herself up out of my embrace and lifts her face to mine, her green eyes are red-rimmed and her nose a bright pink.

I reach behind her back and grab a handful of tissues, handing them to her. She blows her nose and turns her shoulders away.

"Thank you. Gah, I should be the one taking care of you right now, yet here you are"—she flutters her hand in the air between us—"taking care of me. What a mess I am."

"Nah, it's all good. I don't mind."

And oddly enough, I don't mind it at all. There's a comfort level between us. A connection.

Silent moments go by until she finally speaks again, her voice barely a whisper and her words accompanied by chirpy hiccups.

"When I saw you lying motionless on the ice...it broke something in me that I've managed to keep glued together all these months as I've dealt with Marv's condition." Her shoulders slump forward and she drops her chin to her chest. I rub her back in a soothing motion, tucking her fallen hair behind her ear. "Seeing you all sprawled out unconscious? I think it brought up all the fears I've carried around with me about losing Marv. I was scared shitless that you wouldn't get up. That...*you'd*..."

"End up in a coma?"

She twists her head so her worried eyes meet mine. "Or worse. God, it was terrifying. The whole event keeps replaying in my head."

"Karis, it's okay. Look at me, I'm fine." I motion with my hands over my body. Granted, my head hurts and I'll still have to go through some neurological testing, but I'm no worse for wear.

Karis gives me a once-over and then gets to her feet. She begins to pace at the end of the bed, pivoting on her heels and repeating the process. She's back to her *don't fuck with me* brilliance and offers me a look that says, *it's not okay, idiot.'*

"Do you mind telling me what you saw? What happened exactly?" I don't want to upset her further but wanting it'd help to get the play-by-play from a firsthand witness if possible. "I don't remember much of what happened, only that Russo had been hurling insults at me through the entire first period, trying to get under my skin, but I didn't play along."

"Hey old man, you need a cane to go with those skates?"

"Is that the best you got? Old? At least I'm not fucking ugly, Russo."

I snort at the memory. There was a lot more of that, but nothing prepared me for that dirty penalty against the boards.

Karis takes a seat on a chair in the corner of the room, a few feet from the bed and with a long inhalation, she expels the air through her mouth like she's practicing a yoga technique.

I get myself comfortable once more, fluffing the pillows behind me and keeping my eyes trained on Karis. She closes her eyes and massages her temple.

"Kip told me how much Russo dislikes you."

I laugh wryly. "That's putting it mildly."

"I'm not sure what's between you two or how far back it goes, but what he did? It wasn't about playing hockey." She casts her eyes down to the floor and shakes her head. When she lifts her gaze back and I see her concern and resolve.

"He was trying to end your career."

18

K aris

Ballas sucks in deep breath, letting it out slowly as he rubs a palm over his temple.

"Yeah, I kinda get that now. The shit Russo pulled tonight was uncalled for." Ballas kicks off the sheet and clasps his hands behind his head to lean against the pillows. "Will you tell me exactly what you saw?"

I give him a nod and check my phone, hoping to have received a follow-up to my request by now from Nate McGowan.

While Ballas was getting his things together in the locker room after the game and getting well wishes from his team-mates, I immediately went to see Nate in his office and told him to contact the commissioner and relay my message.

"I want the league to know that what Sergei Russo did to Keeney is unacceptable and I expect them to take action," I'd said sharply, brooking no argument.

For once Nate seemed to be on the same page with me. To say we've butt heads since I took over from my uncle is an understatement. There's always an underlying current of misogyny in the way he responds to me. Sometimes it's the way he glowers at me when he thinks I'm not looking, other times it's the slight digs and condescending remarks that border on being rude and disrespectful.

I've let them slide for the most part because, truthfully, I'm a novice at this game and as a woman, I don't want to seem like a whiny brat who can't handle the locker room talk linked with professional sports. I've been forced to rely on Nate and his staff to educate me, just as I did with Marek when I took over the Pilots team several years ago.

But tonight, I know what I witnessed, and it was flagrant. The minute I saw Ballas's head snap against the glass, his body ricocheting from the boards and falling to the ice, I knew the hit should result in something bigger than just a penalty.

"Russo does not deserve to play another day on our ice or any other ice until his actions are dealt with properly."

And now as I tell Ballas what I saw, my temper flares once more on the type of swift and just punishment the league should give Sergei Russo.

"It all happened so fast. One minute you got the pass and you're flying down the ice before passing it off to Costa, the crowd all cheering because Costa is owning it on the break-away. The next moment, Sergei pummels you into the boards. You haven't had the puck for seconds, so you didn't expect the hit." I pause and lift my hand to chest as I recall the image in my head that stole my breath away. "Your skates literally left the ice, your body slammed into the boards, and you fell in a motionless heap."

Ballas closes his eyes and grimaces in pain. I get up from my chair and put a hand on his shoulder.

"Are you okay? Can I get you some more pain reliever?"

Ballas's hand covers mine with a gentle squeeze. "It's all good. I just don't remember any of that, so it's a bit alarming, that's all."

Speaking of alarm, the doorbell chimes down the hallway with the order I'd placed twenty minutes ago. I'd let the doorman know to let the delivery guy in.

"That's our dinner. I'll be right back."

I open the door to accept the food and bring it into the kitchen. I pull out plates and utensils and dish up the fragrant food, the tomato and garlic scent reminding me of trip to Italy my uncle too me on as a high-school graduation gift.

Marv purchased the Vikings right after that trip and then bought this condo.

The condo is open and beautiful, with a grand staircase that leads up to a master suite overlooking Stanley Park, the West Vancouver skyline, and the Burrard Inlet. It's an incredible view and on sunny days with the mountains in the background, it's even more magnificent.

Tonight, the lights of the downtown skyline twinkle from afar and the mist on the windows left by the rain makes them sparkle like tiny diamonds.

"Smells delicious."

I startle, my gaze darts to the hallway to see Ballas walking toward me.

"Hey, you're supposed to stay in bed," I grouse, placing the plate on a tray. "I was going to bring this to you."

He snorts. "There are only two things I like to do in bed. Eating is not one of them. Unless, of course, it's to feast on your..."

The tray I've prepared wobbles in my hands, the sound of the glasses clinking together stops him from finishing the sentence. I can't look at him and instead put the food down on the table.

"Then I guess we'll eat out here in the dining room."

Ballas takes a seat at the end of the table. I avoid opening that can of worms by focusing on placing the food in front of him and avoiding his perceptive gaze.

"Thanks. This looks good."

"My grandmother used to say soup is good for what ails you," I say, handing him a spoon for the minestrone I ordered as the starter. His fingers brush over my knuckles when he takes it and a streak of lightning bolts up my arm.

I ignore the chemical reaction and take the corner seat, placing the napkin on my lap before picking up my own spoon. I submerge it into the steamy hot soup and extract a heaping spoonful, blowing on the contents to cool it off before I take a bite.

"There are other things I think could be good for what ails me." His words are provocative and potent.

I lick my lips as I notice where his pulse flickers fast in the side of his neck.

God, this man is so irritatingly handsome.

I snick. "Do I need to remind you of your concussion?"

"Just telling it like it is. Head injury or not, it doesn't diminish my attraction to you, sweetheart."

The look in his eyes is molten hot. Hotter than the soup.

I set my spoon down in the bowl and tilt my head. "Are you always this way with women, Ballas? Always so forward about sex?"

He seems to think on this for a minute, raising his eyebrows and then peers seductively at me. That look from his dark gray eyes could render any woman speechless and probably pantyless.

I wish things were simple between us. Where we were just a man and a woman with an insane attraction to each other and we could do something about it.

Because I would throw caution to the wind if it wouldn't land me in a compromising position. I would let him into my bed in an instant with no regrets.

Unfortunately, those issues can't be resolved tonight, not while he's here dealing with a head injury, and I'm still in charge of the Vikings franchise.

"I have been known to flirt and to say what's on my mind." His gaze meets mine and my heart flips in my chest. The low timbre in his voice sends tingles through my belly. "But it goes beyond that with you, princess."

"Why do you call me that? I'm not a princess."

Ballas runs a hand over his jawline. "You're definitely an heiress and I'd consider you kind of hockey world royalty. Tell you what," he offers, tapping a finger against his chin. "I promise I won't call you princess...in *public*. How's that?"

I roll my eyes and sniff. "You're so bad. Don't strain yourself."

He leans in closer and I feel a bead of sweat roll down my back from the heat of this attraction. "I agree with you there. I've been known to be very, *very* bad."

Deciding this conversation needs to be stopped before I end up doing something I regret, I take a bite of soup and swallow to get a breather.

"Have you spoken to Marek recently?"

Ballas lifts his spoon to his lips and then sets it back in his bowl and wipes away some remnants from the corners of his mouth.

"Not since before training camp. But I did get a chance to spend a little time with him and Harper this summer. I stayed at their place and we did some hiking in the Cascades and golfing out in Sammamish."

"I heard you did some fishing in the Gulf, too. Did you go alone?"

Very smooth, Karis. Even a concussed man can see right through that question.

Ballas lifts his brows. "Hmm, interested in my extracurricular activities, princess?"

"No." The word comes out too quickly and I feel the heat painting across my cheeks. "I happened to overhear it while Marek and I were in a meeting in his office. And no, I wasn't trying to get the latest on your extracurriculars then either. I don't care what you do outside of hockey."

"You're a terrible liar."

I look away and down at my plate. It's embarrassing to be so transparent but I deny it nonetheless. "I am not."

"You lied the other night when you said you don't want to sleep with me." Ballas stands up and moves to tower over me. I hesitate before tilting my head back to stare up into this beast's hot and dark eyes.

He grips me at the shoulders and pulls me to my feet. I feel weightless, bound to obey him without putting up a fight.

He cups a hand around my throat, squeezing gently as he strokes his thumb at the underside of my chin. Shivers bolt down my spine.

"Admit it. You lied when you said you didn't want to sleep with me again."

My breath stalls as he drags the pad of his thumb over my bottom lip, hypnotizing me with his touch.

My lips part and I swipe his thumb with my tongue.

"I can't."

He cocks his brow. "You can't what, princess?"

I give an imperceptible shake of my head. My voice sounds breathy, clearly communicating my desire even if I can't.

"I can't say that."

He pushes his whole thumb into my mouth, depressing my tongue, and my jaw opens to obey him.

"Suck, sweetheart."

Those words. That gesture. My panties go damp and my clit throbs at the course words.

I close my eyes and succumb to the bold request, sucking his thumb deep as my cheeks hollow in and out. Suddenly, Ballas's hands grasps my hips, and in one fluid motion he pulls me against him. I feel his erection bulging hard as steel inside his shorts. He swings me around so my stomach presses against the table and bends me over, grabbing both my wrists to stretch me out. My cheek is flat against the wood of the tabletop and his mouth is at my ear.

"Say you've thought about me fucking you again, princess." With a tilt of his hips, Ballas grinds against my ass. A moan releases from my chest. "Don't lie to me."

I tug one hand free and slip it behind my back to wedge between our bodies and cup his thick cock in my palm. He jerks in surprise and hisses out in pleasure as I rub my hand roughly over his arousal.

"I am not. A. Liar," I say through gritted teeth, the truth finally able to be set free. "I think about it all the time."

19

―――――

B allas

I'd like to blame it on my concussion but that's a cop out.

I have no control when I'm with this woman.

It's grown like a wildfire in a dry field. Every time I'm near her, it grows.

With her hand at my crotch, Karis has awoken the beast inside me, and I'm desperate to take this further.

My shorts are in the way of her quest. I undo the tie at the front and slide them down my hips, bending at the waist to kick them off at my ankles. Karis flips around and stares down at my impressive erection and licks her lips.

"That kind of reaction will get you in trouble, princess." I run my palm over my hard-on.

"You seem to bring out the bad girl in me," she murmurs in a sexy whisper, tugging at my briefs. The minute my cock springs free, her fingers lace around it in a tight grip, and she strokes me hard.

My cock twitches in her grasp. It's been far too long since I've had any fingers other than my own wrapped around my shaft.

I almost feel lightheaded at the sensation.

My knees go weak and wobbly and my vision does this weird zig-zaggy dance.

Oh fuck.

My vision suddenly becomes blurry around the edges and the room begins to spin—and it's not from the very welcome hand job she's giving me.

I draw in a breath, hoping oxygen will do its job and restore my stability.

No such luck.

I slam my palm against the table and wave her hand off my dick.

She stares at me like she's seen a ghost.

"Oh my God. Sit down, Ballas, quick," she blurts, yanking out a chair from the table. "Head between your legs." That is definitely not the head I want between my legs.

She drops her hands to my hips and guides me to the chair, where I plop down with an unceremonious thud.

I lower my head between my knees and groan.

I'm semi-naked with a semi-chub and about to pass out in front of a woman.

"This is a first," I chuckle dryly. "It's not usually my own thighs my head is between."

"Hush. Hold on. I'll get you a wet washcloth."

I hear Karis pad into the kitchen and turns on the faucet. A few moments later I feel a wet washcloth on the back of my neck. The cool interruption against my hot skin, along with the tips of her fingers grazing my neckline, has me breaking out with goosebumps.

"Goddamn it, Ballas," she curses. "What were we thinking? You're in no condition to do this. The doctor specifically said no physical assertion. That includes any sexual activities. God, how could I let you do that?"

I tug the washcloth away and slowly straighten, testing my vision by staring straight ahead and blinking a few times. The buzz has dissipated and there's no more fuzziness in my peripheral vision but the ego-busting embarrassment lingers.

"You know, ten years ago, I could have run a marathon and fucked hard even under these conditions. Now I can't even get a handy without passing out. Jesus, I really am an old fucking man."

Karis squats in front of me, a smile forming at the corners of her mouth, her eyebrows softening in understanding. I know I shouldn't admit any of this to her. It only makes me look vulnerable in her eyes. Beasts are not to be seen as weak.

Gentle hands squeeze my knees. "This does not in any way make you frail or old. You've experienced major head trauma, compounded by previous concussions. It has nothing to do with your age, size, or very healthy libido." She smirks. "Sometimes a little too healthy."

She winks and lifts her eyebrows appreciatively, her eyes dancing with humor.

"It's still fucking embarrassing as hell."

Karis hands me my shorts, which I slip over my feet and up my legs as I stand. She takes a step back and drops her arms, giving me space.

"Do you know it took me six months after my accident and back surgeries before I could fully walk again on my own?"

I shake my head, following her without resistance as she leads me back into the bedroom with an arm slung around my hips.

"I first walked on a treadmill with this contraption that hooked me in and kept me upright. I slowly graduated to a walker, then a cane, until I could finally move without assistance. It was the worst time of my life. I hated that my friends saw me like that. It was devastating for a sixteen-year-old's psyche."

I throw back the covers and slide into bed. Karis sits down in the same spot she was earlier.

"That must've been tough. But look at you now." I give her an appreciative smile.

"Yes. Look at me now. And in a few weeks, you'll be able to run that marathon again and do all the things you so badly want to do." She blushes and turns away.

"Say it, princess." I prod, a hint of amusement returning at how cute she looks when the topic of sex arises.

I grab her wrist and tug her down so I can slide my lips from her cheekbone to her ear.

"*Fuck*. The word is fuck. And believe me, I want to fuck *you*, and sooner rather than later."

I fall asleep minutes after making this bold statement.

WHEN I AWAKEN twelve hours later, light streams into the room and the smell of coffee and breakfast wafts through the crack in the door Karis must have left open.

A smile turns up at the corners of my mouth. My guess is Karis poked her head in every few hours last night to check on me throughout the night just like the doctor said to do.

Such a good girl.

My dick stirs in my shorts at the unbidden dirty thoughts I have from the idea of her obeying me. I throw my legs over the side of the bed and stretch. My body creaks and cracks with the sounds of a veteran hockey player. The aches and pains are nothing, however, compared to the agonizing thought of my future me if I'm not given the green light to play again.

I think of the greats in the game and what they accomplished post-career. Gretzky. Bobby Orr. Mario Lemieux. I'm not nearly as famous and will never rack up the kind of points they did, but I've hopefully left a big enough mark with the Vikings to have my number sent into the arena's rafters .

Retired. The word leaves me with a gaping hole of uncertainty.

A soft knock on the door draws my attention from my pity session and I drag my gaze from the floor where I'd been staring into space up to Karis. She looks ravishing in an oversized cream Vikings sweatshirt and tight-fitting leggings, her blonde hair pulled back into a high pony tail at the top of her head. Casual and understated. I've never seen her looking so fresh and comfortably sexy.

But let me tell you, she looks fucking fantastic in everything.

"Good morning." She smiles, her eyes generously flitting over my bare chest. I tugged off my T-shirt last night when I grew too warm so now I'm only in my briefs. "I just wanted to let you know I made some breakfast if you're up for it. Since you didn't get to finish dinner last night."

My stomach takes the opportunity to rumble loudly and I chuckle, making to stand from the bed and remembering my balance is still a little weak. I wobble like a bender when I stand up.

I sit back down and throw the shirt over my head. Karis hands me the shorts I'd discarded last night.

"Thanks. Breakfast sounds good." She nods and turns, heading out the door while I finish getting dressed.

Karis.

If the situation was reversed, would I step up and take care of her like she has for me?

Probably not. It's not a natural tendency of mine to think of another's needs above my own. Much to my mother's chagrin, I've never been in a relationship where I've had to be responsible for another person, except for my hockey brothers.

Even within my own family, my mother was always the one who took care of the house for my dad and my younger siblings while I was growing up. Now, I've lived solo for so long now I've gotten used to my single lifestyle. I've never even had as much as a goldfish to be accountable to. Until now, I've enjoyed being on my own.

Most of my teammates settled down and got married young. I never felt I would be good at balancing a career in hockey —playing 82 games a year with road trips and travel—and having a family to care for. Honestly, I don't know how the guys like Nils and Canny and others married with kids manage the distraction in their lives.

I get to my feet again, this time with a greater degree of stability. Maybe a bit more slowly than usual, but I walk down the hallway to the kitchen, noticing Karis's laptop and a pile of paperwork out on the dining room table. "Already hard at work, I see."

She swings her head over her shoulder. "I've been on the line with Nate and the commissioner this morning."

Karis lifts two plates from the counter and places them in the same spots at the table where we ate dinner last night. The exact spot where I attempted—and failed miserably— to fuck a very willing and eager woman.

I clear my throat and glance down at the plethora of delicious-smelling food.

"Thanks. This looks great."

"You're welcome."

"Hey, Karis," I say, before starting in on the breakfast she's prepared. She looks up, her face fresh and free from any makeup. It makes her look younger than she is. She could pass for a college student easier than as an owner of a billion-dollar hockey franchise. "I just wanted to say thank you. I know I've put you in a difficult spot."

I don't need to expound on that sentiment. The look she gives me tells me everything I already know.

"It's complicated, I'll admit," she says and her eyes flutter. "But remember, I made this decision and I'm happy to do it."

I take a few bites, allowing for Karis to enjoy her breakfast before I ask her the question that's on my mind this morning. Where do things stand with the determination on Sergei's dirty hit?

And when can I return to the ice?

20

Karis

It's been so long since I've had breakfast with a man who wasn't Marv, business associates, or part of my management teams.

Ballas looks even sexier than I expected in the morning. I could get used to him sitting here at the breakfast table with his messy dark hair, and his warm, musky scent spinning me up with thoughts of returning to bed with him, leaving breakfast to wait. I have to keep my eyes focused on my veggie omelet to prevent them from wandering over his handsome features where I'm sure he'd easily read my lustful thoughts.

I can't help sneaking a peek between my lashes to see his unshaven jawline that's scruffy with stubble, moving up and down as he chews. Although he now wears a T-shirt and track pants, I conjure up the image of his toned physique that I salivated over earlier in the bedroom.

Stop. It's a ridiculous fantasy.

Wishing for more of what Ballas was offering last night is stupid and will get me nowhere. If it were a tied hockey game, there'd be extra time so someone could win. But with us, the circumstances are hopeless.

I have too much power over his future career to get involved with him.

After a few bites, my gaze drifts to find him staring at me.

"Do you plan on filling me in on Russo and what the league decided? Or should I wait for lunch?" His tone is teasing but the message clear. Hurry up, Karis and get to the point.

I roll my eyes.

"Oh, that?" I wave my hand in dismissal but I can't keep the humor out of my tone. "You're far too weak right now. I'd hate for the stress to upset you."

I press my lips together to hide my smile.

"*Karrrrrissss…*" he cajoles with a meaningful look.

"Okay, fine. You win." I put down my fork and wipe my mouth with the napkin. Ballas does the same and props his elbows on the table, leaning forward to give me his full attention. "Nate and I exchanged emails and then had a phone call early this morning with NHL Commissioner Jones. The league officials and Player Safety committee have reviewed the hit and determined a three-game suspension for Russo is warranted."

"Motherfuckers," Ballas bellows making me blanch.

"I thought you'd be happy with that outcome?"

Ballas pushes back from the table and strides over to the windows of the condo. His broad shoulders stiffen and he folds his arms over his chest, his back muscles tensing visibly under his shirt.

"Happy?" he snaps, his voice laced with irritation. "Fuck no. Russo isn't the type to learn from this stunt. He'll continue to push the limits until he injures someone for life."

Ballas is right, of course. But there's not much more that can be done. The league has its Player Safety and union policies in place for things like this, just like the NBA situation with Hammond Greis's alleged domestic violence. There are safeguards in place and the team, management, and the league itself have only so much latitude to enforce the rules.

He swings his body back around, his expression softening. "Sorry. I didn't mean to go off. It just pisses me the fuck off that his time served"—he uses air quotes—"is likely the same amount of time I'll likely be out. He'll have equal opportunity this season to keep up with my stats."

"Ahh," I note with a nod. "So, it all comes back to some competitive rivalry thing between you two. I see now."

Ballas takes a seat again and finishes his food, scarfing it down and shaking his head in a manner that says I have no idea what I'm talking about. And maybe I don't. I've never been in competition over anything, except maybe with myself.

After my parents died in the accident, my only goal was to get back on my feet. I wasn't going to let anything more disrupt my life. I was laser-focused on my physical recovery and nothing and no one would get in the way.

I suppose it's the same with Ballas. He's a driven player. From what I've seen, Ballas puts everything into hockey. A man who tries to knock him down, like Russo did, doesn't stand a chance.

Hockey is his life. And until he's able to be back out doing what he loves, he feels helpless and aimless, which makes me wonder what Ballas will do after his contract expires and he becomes a free agent.

"What will you do when you can't play professional hockey anymore?" The words slip off my tongue before I realize I'm even asking them out loud.

Ballas rears back, his gaze pinning me with something I can't read. They turn dark and a muscle quivers in his jaw.

"Why would you ask me that?"

"Well..." I stammer, unprepared for his resistant reaction. I suppose it makes sense. Why would he share his plans with me? But I feel we've moved past that typical working relationship. We've been intimate and share an attraction that goes well beyond flirtatious, but I can understand his reticence. "I didn't mean anything by it. I'm just curious what you've thought of doing once you retire."

"Sounds like you're already talking to Coach Thomas to bench my ass and take me off the roster."

I place my hand on his forearm. It flexes underneath my palm.

"God, no. That's not what I meant. I was actually curious. Have you ever considered coaching or managing a team at some level?"

Ballas snorts at this suggestion. "Me? Manage a team? Probably not in my wheelhouse."

Leaning back in my chair, I fold my arms over my chest and tilt my head to the side, mentally checking off the reasons I think he'd be great in that role while I lock my eyes with his.

"For one, you're college educated and have plenty of experience working in the league with a variety of personality traits. You seem to get along and play well with others."

A loud grunt of disagreement from Ballas. "I'm an asshole who doesn't filter shit."

I dismiss him with a wave. "I've also seen how you've worked with the rookies and prospects during training camp. You're very good with giving direction. What about coaching?"

"Oh, I like giving direction all right..." His voice deepens to that low and sensual tone of his. "But in the bedroom is where I enjoy it most."

Holy Lord, don't I know it. I can't help the heat that blooms up my neck and over my cheeks as I recall exactly how good he is at that too.

"Spread your legs, sweetheart."

"That's it. Suck my cock like a good girl."

"No disputing that," I insist, rising from the chair to clear the breakfast dishes from the table. "Maybe you could do both."

I take the dishes to the kitchen and start rinsing off the plates at the sink. Ballas follows and steps in behind me, caging me in with his hands on the counter's edge and pressing his body flush to mine.

"Or, maybe I could just do you."

My arm swims with goosebumps as his fingers skate over my flesh. I close my eyes and enjoy the warmth of his touch, my body soaking it in like the dry earth after a rain.

Then his fingers dip further and with a teasing flutter, he moves over the edge of my waistband.

"I want you, Karis." One finger nudges underneath the elastic, testing the water, and I suck in a breath. When I don't stop him, Ballas burrows inside and slips his hand into my panties. "And I'm about to find out how wet I make you. You're not the boss right now."

I sag against him with an exhale and drop my head back to rest at his shoulder, no longer able to resist this desire for him that's burned inside me for ages.

"I'm going to fuck you with my fingers, princess. Will you let me?"

I grip the counter with my fingers and groan.

"Yes. Please."

"Good girl."

B allas

I slide my fingers into her panties, over her slit and find her already soaked. A deep growl escapes my throat.

"You're already wet for me."

Karis lets out a soft moan in response and lord help me my dick swells. I press my lips to the intoxicating skin of her neck, breathing in her scent that makes me dizzy. This time, I know it's not my head spinning me up. It's all her.

I run my tongue over the expanse of her taut flesh, savoring her sensual flavor. I roam up to her ear lobe and bite it between my teeth.

"I'm going to make you come...but I'll give you the choice." I curl the tip around the shell of her ear and flick it. "Either my fingers or my tongue."

She whimpers a sound of encouragement as I swirl both my tongue and my fingers. Her hips buck against my hand.

"Both?"

I chuckle darkly at her breathy response and consider our location. With a quick perusal of the kitchen counter, I drop my hands, lift her in my arms, and swing her up onto the flat surface of the kitchen bar that bisects the kitchen and dining area.

The buzz of sexual need courses through my blood stream. I skim my hands up the inside of her thighs, toying with the hem before slipping my fingers under her shirt and flattening my hand over her stomach. I glide my fingers over the flat of her belly, enjoying the way it concaves when she sucks in a sexy breath.

Just because I can, I lean down and circle her belly button with my tongue, dipping inside as she trembles and moans in pleasure. I make a wet trail upward toward her breasts as goose bumps form along the way. When I reach the outline of one pebbled nub poking through her bra, I skate patterns over the lace with my finger, followed by a flick of my tongue.

With Karis lying flat on the surface of the counter, my erection nestles perfectly at the juncture of her spread legs. I grind my hips against her pussy, the heat from her driving me wild. God what I wouldn't give to bury myself inside her right this minute.

Knowing it's out of the question, I return my attention to her supple tits, full and plump. I cup them in my palms and roll my thumbs over the stiff peaks of her nipples.

"Fucking perfect." I murmur before I wrench the cups of her bra down and her tits pop free.

Karis lets out a torn cry when I take one of her nipples between my teeth and suck it hard, tugging the beaded nub inside my mouth.

Karis laces her fingers through the strands of hair at the back of my head, tugging roughly to extract a groan from me. The sensation sends a wave of pleasure down to my swollen cock. I sweep my tongue over each distended nipple and squeeze her plump breasts.

Then I work my way back down her core, using the scruff from my beard to score over her sensitive flesh until I reach the top of her leggings. I tug them off with ease, removing her panties along with them. She kicks them off her ankles and I'm treated to the most beautiful sight.

My gaze is now centered on her bare pussy glistening with wetness. When I peer back up at Karis's face, her eyes are closed and her lips parted.

"Eyes open and down here, princess. You're going to watch me fuck your pussy with my fingers and my mouth just like you ordered."

Karis's eyes fly open and connect with mine. They smolder with desire as she bites down on her lower lip.

I drag my thumb through her sex and bring it to my mouth, licking the pad to taste what I've been missing for so long. Her eyes grow wide and her lips part with a slack jaw.

"You want a taste, princess?" I give her a sexy grin, offering her my thumb like a gift to a queen.

Her lips wrap around my thumb without hesitation and the suction of her mouth has my cock twitching in desperation for what it wants and needs.

I lightly strum over her sensitive clit, increasing the pressure as I circle the pulsing nub. Karis squirms under my ministrations until I finally slide a finger inside her wet entrance. The glorious tight heat I find when I thrust in has me gritting my teeth in need. Her grip on my hair tightens and her body jerks in response each time I sink and withdraw my finger. When I add a second, I swirl and scissor, finding a rhythm to exact her pleasure.

"Ballas," she hisses out the moment I withdraw my fingers and my mouth takes their place. "Oh my God…"

I simply growl like an animal at her wet heat. With each stroke of my tongue, my mouth floods with her taste. It makes me want to whip out my cock and slam into her, fucking her hard and fast until we are both dizzy with pleasure and reaching for that high.

That's what I would normally do. The denial of pleasure for me is almost unbearable, something I've never had to suffer through before. I'm usually on a quest to fuck until we're both screaming out our releases.

With Karis, it's not the usual fuck and run. It's Karis's pleasure and orgasm that are paramount to me right now. My only goal is to make her come hard against my mouth and cry out my name as she does.

Karis drives me even harder to ensure her satisfaction and give her the best fucking orgasm she's ever experienced.

I let out a determined groan and work my tongue inside her snug pussy.

Holy hell.

When she cries outs a plea, I lose myself and set out on a mission to score.

I vacillate between soft, feather-light strokes and making long drags of the flat of my tongue over her slit. She grips and grasps, groans and grinds. When I plunge my tongue inside her heat, she clenches her thighs against my ears and her strangled whisper tells me she's close.

"Ballas...don't stop."

My fingers curl inside her pussy as I suck her sweet clit between my teeth. When I find that soft spot of hers, I experiment with a slow thrust, groaning from the tight heat that sheaths my fingers. Her arousal on my tongue is consuming, but the slick, wet slide of her pussy is magical.

Karis rocks against me, fingers latched in my hair, and lets go with a long scream of pleasure. I smile against her wet pussy as I feel her body shutter and strain with the rapture of her release.

I lift my head from between her legs and run a hand across my mouth, her taste and scent a flavor I will forever remember. My gaze travels up to Karis's face, where I find her staring at me in something close to wonder.

I quirk an eyebrow, offering my hand to help her sit upright.

Still naked below the waist, her legs dangling at my sides, Karis glances around as if she has no idea how she got to where she did.

"You okay there, princess?" I give her a sly grin. "You seem a little dazed."

Karis blinks and stammers. "That was...oh shit. I can't believe I let you do that."

I'm about to lean in and kiss her when her expression changes, her green eyes flashing something unreadable, like a mix of regret and irritation. I'm confused by the sudden swing in her mood.

Instead of opening her arms for the embrace, Karis pushes against my chest until I'm forced to move back a step. She jumps from the counter, her bare feet landing with a soft thud on the floor. I help her gather the discarded clothing and she clutches the pile protectively in her arms as she tries to dart away from me.

Where the hell is she going?

I reach for her hand to keep her from running off.

"Karis, what just happened here?"

Swinging around, she locks her eyes on mine.

"I lose myself around you, Ballas. I crossed the line I promised myself I wouldn't cross. I allowed myself to...*goddammit.*" Her voice is fiery and borders on frantic. She flicks away from my grasp and waves at the counter. Then she slips her feet into her leggings and tugs them up her legs. "This is so wrong. You're supposed to be on bedrest with no physical activity, and I just let you...*do* that with your sexual sorcery!"

I chuckle uneasily at her choice of words, rolling my hand over my bearded chin, uncertain how to get back to where we just were.

"Do you mean, make you come? I didn't realize that was witchcraft." I snicker and move my body to back her against the counter. I plant my hands on both sides of her hips and try to figure this woman out. "I thought it was just my skillful tongue."

As far as conversations go, this is not at all what I expected. Then again, Karis is kind of unexpected in every way and keeps me on my toes. She defies a label.

Huffing with indignation, Kari stares up at me, frustration glowing like emeralds in the moonlight in the depths of her eyes. She points an accusatory finger in the air. "Argh! See? You're doing it again."

I lean down and cup her cheeks in my roughened hands, bringing her gaze to rest on mine.

My lips are inches from hers.

"Karis, I would do that again and again and not live to regret it for a second."

My mouth covers hers and I kiss the soft fullness of her lips. My tongue brushes over the bottom lip and I capture her mouth as if searching for an answer neither of us seem to have about this predicament.

When I finally step back, my fingers remain locked around her jaw and I stare into her eyes with a lethal certainty.

There is no denying this is going to happen. Under Karis's all-business disguise, she's a vulnerable woman who brings out the beast in me. A man who wants to protect and comfort her. To be there for her.

To love her.

"Karis, don't fight this," I declare in a harsh whisper. "You can let go with me. I'm yours to use."

22

———

K aris

"How's he doing today, Daria?"

I hate that I haven't been down to Seattle for over a week now to visit Marv, but I've had to remain in Vancouver with the new hockey season in full swing.

Liar.

I've stayed here for another reason. His name is Ballas Keeney.

I do check in on Marv every morning when Daria is there to get an update on his status though. It's also a way for me to chat with Daria, who has become such a confidant for me during this transition.

Daria hums into the phone. "Oh, sweetie, nothing has changed. His vitals were a little low, O2 dipped overnight, and it looks like he may have a kidney infection. I'll monitor his urine output today and of course we'll get him on antibiotics if needed. Otherwise, he's stable."

I anxiously bite my fingernail as if it's done something to anger me.

Daria is fully aware of my feelings on keeping Marv comfortable and healthy as long as we can and has never once suggested I'm not doing the right thing.

We've had gut-wrenching conversations about what it means to keep him on this type of life support long-term. Most people with a family member in state would proceed with a plan to end the life support. I know this and have weighed the pros and cons. Which is why I promised myself I'd give it a year in the hope that he might show some signs of improvement. If he develops any problematic conditions that require intervention, I will make the call then.

There is no greater burden than having the life of someone you love in your hands. The decision has consequences I'm not yet ready to deal with unless the situation is so dire there is no other option.

"Thank you, Dar."

"Honey, you know you're more than welcome. He's in good hands. Speaking of which, I had the sports news on this morning for your uncle and saw that one of your players was injured in the game last night. Ballas something-or-other?"

Hearing his name transmits little shock waves to my heart and a zap of heated sensation to my core.

I clear my throat, hoping my voice sounds normal and not dreamy and smitten like a schoolgirl with a crush.

"Yes, Ballas Keeney, one of our D-men but it's nothing serious. He just needs a bit of rest before going back to the ice."

I'm sure Dar can read between the lines, and although I trust her implicitly with my uncle, I'm unable to share the specific injury details of any of our players. If other teams or the press got wind of the injury, it could show a weakness to be exploited. That's why, in all our press releases, we simply indicate whether the player suffered an upper or lower body injury and their expected duration on the injured reserve list.

In Ballas's case, we've left it as week-to-week, based on his progress.

"And are you getting the rest you need, my dear? I don't want you to overtax yourself." She pauses and I hear the beeps of the heart monitor and the whoosh of air from the ventilator in the background. These are sounds that roam in my head and keep me up at night with worry. "Well, I should let you get back to your work. And the patient is going to get a sponge bath today. I'll see you next week?"

"I'll do my best. Talk to you soon."

My heart sinks as I end the call. I sit down in my chair and drop my chin to my chest, staring down at my feet as I lament over this horrible situation.

But something inexplicably amazing happens that lifts my grief. Instead of getting mired in my troubles, I recall the image of Ballas between my bare thighs, and the way his mouth and fingers brought me to climax earlier this morning. It was a euphoric high that left me flooded with new emotions.

I just wish I hadn't spiraled out of control into an emotional outburst, ruining the moment and my afterglow immediately afterwards.

I left a stunned and confused Ballas in the kitchen, my lips still burning from that searing kiss he gave me, then retreated to the home office. I told him I had to work and I'd check on him in a while.

The work excuse was legitimate because my workweek is never truly over. It may be a Sunday morning but during hockey season, I've quickly learned these roles don't give me any pause to rest.

Coach Thomas and the team flew out to Calgary this morning to start a short road trip, leaving Ballas on the injured reserve list. It also meant Nate and I spoke about who we'd use to replace Ballas while he's out and the plans he and Coach have to finesse the roster.

The entire conversation made me more and more convinced that Nate needs to go. His leadership style is abrupt and dictator-like. It's his way or no way. Honestly, I don't know how Marv handled Nate's behavior when he was running things.

Nate thinks he knows best about everything to do with the club and that I should just accept it as the dumb, rich, blonde girl he takes me for.

Well, he's barking up the wrong bitch if he thinks I'm going to allow him to treat me like that.

Even during our earlier conversation, he didn't like that I disagreed with him about the changes to the roster.

"With Ballas out for a minimum of three games, we should put him on waivers now. He'll be useless to us if he comes back. Recall Stolley to fill our gap."

I clutch the phone in my hand so hard, the glass nearly cracks.

"The analysis isn't there to back your logic, Nate, and I disagree with you. I'm making the executive decision to give Ballas his spot back when he is given the green light to return."

Nate sneers derisively into the phone. "Your analysis..." he seethes. "Numbers aren't everything, Karis. I know the game of hockey. I know what's down the road for him because I've seen it in situations like these. You know *nothing*."

I let his disrespectful comment slide in favor of silence, letting him stew a little longer as I consider my next move.

I sift through my candy dish and select two red ones, popping the Skittles in my mouth as I wait for him to realize I have him by the balls.

"If Marv were here," he starts snidely, "he'd allow me to do the job I'm paid to do."

The sweetness of the candy gives me the boost I need to respond.

"Thank you, Nate. But Marv *isn't* here and I am. I appreciate your viewpoint but I'm also taking into consideration that Stolley had shoulder surgery at the middle of last season. He's not as fast with the stick, therefore more of a liability than Ballas. We can watch Stolley play the next three games and see what we think and if there is a role for him. But Ballas will return to his spot on the roster once he's been given the go-ahead by our team physicians."

I can hear the grind of Nate's teeth on the other end of the line.

Oh boy, that did not go over well.

Although my decision is based on facts and Ballas's contract, it does give me pause to think what would happen if anyone —Nate in particular—ever found out that Ballas and I are having an affair.

Affair.

That word feels so dirty and not at all accurate to describe the crazy physical attraction we have toward one another.

It's like there's this giant and unbreakable magnetic pull that seems to drive me into his arms at every pass. I could glue myself to the wall and staple my feet to the floor and the moment he walked by I'd naturally gravitate toward him.

I have no illusions about who Ballas is and what he wants. It's purely sexual and nothing more for him. From what I know, he's never had a long relationship and is known in the press as a fuck boy. He leaves a trail of puck bunnies along the way like wins in each city he plays.

Yet I don't feel that Ballas has treated me like some puck bunny to be used and tossed away. I'm still uncertain whether his actions match up with the words her professes. He told me he's here for me and that he wants me to use him for what I need.

I want nothing more than to believe what he says, but has he demonstrated to me that I can lean on him? Not just for sex, but for those other emotional things I am missing in my life.

Regardless, I don't have any intention of pursuing anything with Ballas. I need to keep my resolve strong and my willpower on high alert to fend off my insatiable need for this man.

I need to keep my top priorities in mind: my uncle's health and his team's success.

Outside of that, I will not get distracted by this sexy-as-sin alpha man who just happens to be staying in my guest room.

23

B allas

Boredom is a bitch.

The minute Karis walked away from me, I went into the guest suite, got in the shower, and jerked myself off. Hell, I was so hard for her I busted a nut within three strokes while her taste was still on my tongue.

After that is when the boredom set in. Between Karis working and me being forbidden from watching TV, using my phone, or even reading, my only saving grace was a phone call with Marek.

"Hey, Bal. You okay? I saw the hit you took, brother. It looked vicious."

I can always count on Marek to get to the point. We don't see each other much during our busy seasons, but our friendship is closer than ever. Honestly, I thought it would change once he became involved with and then married Harper. My worries were over nothing because Marek is a rock and as loyal as they come.

I pace along the windows of the guest room like a caged cat looking for a way out. Even my orgasm didn't diminish the constant desire for Karis.

Truth is, nothing has done the trick—the distance I kept during the summer, not hockey, not other women. Nothing has satisfied my craving and need for her.

But she's made it clear. There's a line she doesn't want to cross and is adamant we keep it intact.

I blow out a long breath and run a hand through my still damp hair. I let it grow longer over the summer and have been debating whether to cut it before we get too far into the season. Although, Karis certainly likes to weave her fingers through it and snag it in her grasp.

"Depends on the definition of okay." I laugh dryly, shaking off my thoughts about Karis.

"Well, that sounds ominous. You home? Want me to come up for a day or two?"

Marek knows my entire family is back East. My sister, Bella, tried calling me last night but I let it go to voicemail, and I didn't get a chance to call her back since Karis took away my phone privileges until late this morning.

I debate whether I should tell Marek where I am and who, precisely, is taking care of me. He ascertained through that *I've known you for a fuck-long-time* voodoo shit the morning after his wedding that I'd fucked Karis. At the time, she was only his team's owner and not tied to the Vikings beyond her relationship with Marv, so it didn't really matter.

Now, however, the weight of that personal decision has a bit more impact on my professional life, or hers.

The guilt of not telling him weighs heavy on me, though.

"Nah, man. I'm good. Karis Spurlock made sure I had someone with me last night in case anything happened."

There. That's the God's honest truth, even if I've omitted a portion of it.

I underestimate my friend's shit detector because his next question backs me up against the wall.

"Balls, are you *with* Karis?"

That's a fucking loaded question if I've ever heard one. How the fuck do I answer that?

No, I'm not *with* her. Have I been with her? Do I want to be with her again in the biblical sense?

Fuck yeah, I do.

That's irrelevant though since Karis has said her peace.

I chuckle darkly. "I stayed in her guestroom last night. She's the boss and insisted I not be alone. What could I say?"

"Jesus Christ, Bal. Please tell me you didn't sleep with her again." I know without even seeing him that he has that typical furrow in his forehead right now.

"You think so little of me? Dude, I have a head injury."

He chokes out a laugh. "Yeah, exactly. You've always been a fucking headcase but your dick still works."

I snort out in laughter. He's hit the nail on the head, as per usual. The man knows me better than I know myself sometimes.

"No, I did *not* sleep with her." I stare at the bed where I might have if both my body and my brain been in sync. And if she'd finally given in to the irresistible pull between us.

There's a long pause on the line, and I'm sure Marek is trying to decide whether he believes me or not.

"I swear, I did not sleep with her. I slept in the guest bed, alone like a goddamn invalid."

Marek snorts at my response. "Ballas the Beast is a force to be reckoned with. Which means, as soon as you're cleared, I'm sure you'll be back to the same old antics."

"What can I say? Can't keep a good man down."

A light knock on the door drags my attention to Karis, who stands outside the doorway. She makes a face of regret for interrupting me. I shake my head and smile.

"It's just Marek," I tell her, pointing at the phone. "Hey bro, I gotta go. I think the doctor is here to check me out."

"Okay. Keep me posted." Marek pauses for a moment and then throws the gauntlet down. "And bro...keep your dick in your pants for everyone's sake."

I stare at Karis and lift my brows with a grin, glad she can't hear him on the other end.

"We'll see...thanks for calling."

WITH OUR TEAM doctor on the road for the away game, the NHL sent another league physician to evaluate my symptoms with their testing procedure.

The doctor asks about the symptoms I've experienced and whether I've gotten enough rest. Karis remains in the room with my consent. While she doesn't jump in, she does eyeball me when I leave out the part about that dizzy episode last night.

How would I explain that one? "*Oh, gee, doc. I was getting a handy from my boss and it was so good I nearly passed out.*"

"Have you experienced any headaches, sensitivity to light, ringing in the ears, dizziness, nausea or vomiting, or fatigue?"

I shake my head. "No, sir."

Karis glares at me from the corner of the room, clears her throat, and crosses her arms in that bossy mode of hers.

"I guess I felt a little dizzy last night and had a slight headache," I correct, dipping my head and glaring back at her with a *fine, I admit it* look. "But nothing this morning."

The doctor types in the notes in his laptop and nods his head. "Okay, that's normal. I'll check your pupils to see if they track accordingly. How about your sleep and energy level? Were you restless last night? Have any trouble falling asleep or staying asleep?"

"Not for the reasons you think," I murmur quietly under my breath. The culprit was not a blow to the head that kept me awake half the night, it was having to go to bed with a hard-on caused by the woman sitting over in the corner chair.

"No, sir. Once I got into bed, I slept straight through for twelve hours."

The doctor finishes his notes in my chart and follows it up with another question.

"How about concentration? Any confusion or difficulty focusing or remembering things?"

I wish I could forget the sweet taste of Karis's orgasm on my tongue this morning or the wet slide of my finger inside her pussy. That would make my life a whole lot easier right now. Instead, I seem to be fighting a raging erection at every turn.

"None, although the time right before and after the hit I don't recall. But everything else is good. Would you like me to list off all the provinces of Canada for you? Or recite my childhood home address backwards three times?"

This gets the serious man to chuckle and he pats my knee. "I think that will do for now, Ballas."

Karis finally speaks up. "Dr. Brahma, it's my understanding that these symptoms may evolve over time, even days, after a serious concussion and that continued rest and monitoring is critical for the health of the concussed." She lifts her eyebrows knowingly. "Especially for someone who has a history of concussions."

What the hell is she doing? Is she trying to sabotage my chances of getting back out on the ice? I'm already out for a required three-game hiatus. I don't need her meddling and getting in my way of returning to the ice. Even if she is the boss.

Dr. Brahma stands, stuffing his laptop in the bag and all his instruments away along with it. Then he turns to Karis, his dark eyes filled with sincerity and his tone holding a gentle confidence.

"Based on Ballas's physical and cognitive tests, I don't see any concern with his gradual progression back to more activities…" He knits his brows at me. "That is, unless those activities provoke any of the cognitive and physical symptoms we just covered."

The doctor hands me a form that includes a list of all the physical activities I can add back into my day. The list includes light aerobic exercise with limited head movement and increased heart rate, followed by the progression every 24-hours into more intensity and resistance training.

But all I hear and drill in on from his explanation on physical exertion is *sex*.

When I swivel to look at Karis, it appears that she knows exactly what I'm thinking. Her cheeks bloom with a pink blush.

"Understood," I agree, staring into Karis's eyes with a sly grin.

"And when should we consider him ready to return to play, doctor?" Karis inquires as she leads him toward the front door of the condo.

"That all depends on the club physician and consulting neuropsychologist's clinical review. Ballas must be free of any concussion-related symptoms before engaging in further on-ice activity."

I mentally check off the dates. I should be able to return to the next team practice on Friday morning if everything goes according to plan.

What I'll be doing before then is anyone's guess.

I'd like to think it will involve Karis.

Naked and in bed.

24

———

K aris

"Can I ask you something?"

I've been working at the kitchen table for the past hour after we finished dinner, stewing over my disagreement with Nate from earlier today. I've mulled over all of our past discussions, trying to evaluate objectively whether I think Nate is the right person for this role.

I want to ask Ballas's opinion of the GM before I make a final decision but realize there's a conflict of interest there, considering that Nate wants to cut Ballas and I don't.

However, Ballas is not known for sugarcoating anything and he's worked with Nate long enough to have formed some level of opinion based on his experience. If I make this decision based on solely my own perspective, I'll be doing the team a disservice.

I peek over the top of my laptop to find Ballas sprawled out on the couch, looking casual and comfortable in his track pants and T-shirt as he watches the pre-game sports commentary.

He mutes the TV and swings his head in my direction, giving me his undivided attention.

"If it's about our chances of beating the shit out of Calgary tomorrow, there is no question. We've got this, even if I'm relegated to this couch to watch it play out." He regards me with a smile, flipping to his side and propping his head in his palm. "But go ahead, what's on your mind?"

I hesitate a moment and slowly close my laptop, considering how to ask this without giving away too much. These types of things can swirl in the gossip mill and I don't want it getting out.

"What do you think of Nate McGowan's leadership? What do your teammates say about him?"

The question seems to give him pause, his brow wrinkling. "Hmm...that's a loaded question."

Ballas swings his legs over the side to sit himself upright before bending his long torso at the waist, propping his elbows on his thighs. His biceps flex and pop, and I swallow at the sheer sexiness of this man. Even in the most mundane situations he exudes sexual appeal and does crazy things to my belly.

After the doctor's visit, we came to the joint conclusion that Ballas would remain in my home for another 24 hours. One more night to ensure he's good on his own and solid on his feet before he returns to his own apartment.

Of course, I persuade myself into believing it's purely a business decision and nothing personal.

But that's a lie I've told myself because I've enjoyed his company these last two days. I didn't realize how lonely I'd been and how much I craved the presence of another soul in my midst. Specifically, I've craved Ballas's touch and closeness.

It hasn't come without a great deal of difficulty, though. I have to keep my reactions in check so I don't do something stupid. Like throw off all my clothes and jump him while he's on the couch looking sexy and good enough to eat.

Like now, for example.

Ballas slides his fingers through his tousled hair, the strands sliding softly out of his eyes and long lashes.

He shrugs. "I can't say I think he's made the best decisions for the team, in my opinion. On top of which, he's an A-1 asshole. But that's just my personal bias and means nothing in the grand scheme of things."

I know I can't share my intentions with Ballas, but I do want to test the waters. We had that brief conversation already about Ballas's plans for retirement. Although he didn't sound too interested in managing or coaching a team, I believe he's extremely capable of doing it.

"Your feedback—" I stop and correct myself. "I mean, the *players'* feedback is important. A GM is such a critical piece. A leadership change, like what we did when Marek took over as GM for Pilots, can turn a team from a losing prospect to a winning franchise."

"That's Marek for you. He's a good guy in every way."

I lick my lips. "You're a good guy, too, Ballas."

He huffs. "Not sure that's an adjective anyone has ever used to describe me. I'm grumpy and pissed off most of the time."

"You sell yourself short." My voice is soft but firm as I stand and move into the living room. I take the seat directly across from the couch where he sits, mirroring his position and placing my forearms against the top of my thighs. "I've seen enough of you to know that when you allow yourself the freedom to do it, you're respectful and caring. You certainly have shown that side of yourself with me."

Something flashes in his dark eyes and his jaw tenses. My entire body prickles with awareness of his power and control, capable of turning me into a puddle of pleasure.

In this moment, I am keenly aware of the risk I would take to be with him. I want to throw out all the guidelines and unwritten rules about proprietorship I've tried to follow and show him exactly what he does to me and what he's come to mean to me.

"Karis...I'm warning you. Be careful...because that look on your face makes me want to be anything *but* respectful to you right now."

The honesty in his husky response shoots straight to my core, swirling hot like I just downed a shot of whisky. It sends waves of brazen desire through my bloodstream. It's the key to unlock the door I've kept shut in order to protect myself and keep things professional.

Well, screw that. I'm alone with a man who looks good enough to eat and I want to do just that.

I lower my eyes and flutter my lashes, biting down on my lip with the hope of enticing him without words.

It may have been me who initiated our night in Vegas together last December, but that was a one-off. I'm not normally the instigator in sexual situations. Now that I've learned how dominant Ballas can be—on the ice and in the bedroom—I want to let him take the reins and make the next move.

My voice is a whisper. "I happen to like it when you're like that…"

He blinks, his mouth twitching. "Do you know what you're asking me, princess?"

"Yes," I assert confidently. "Tell me what you want me to do, Ballas and I'll do it. I won't stop it this time."

"*Fuuuuck…*" Ballas drops his head and slams a hand through his hair, running it over his scalp as if the request presents a problem he needs to solve. When his eyes lift to meet mine again, they are as dark as a starless night. They flash danger and it gives me the most potently illicit thrill.

"Fine, if you want to play, I'll play." He points his index finger at the ground and then slides toward the edge of the couch. "On your knees, princess."

The command in his tone sends a streak of desire through me and I immediately slip off the chair's cushion and drop to my knees.

"Good girl. Now hands on the floor and crawl." He crooks the same finger and beckons me forward.

Inch by inch, I grow closer, panting softly with choppy breaths. I move slowly and intentionally toward him until I'm positioned between his open legs.

"Do you know what I had to do this morning while your taste was still on my tongue?"

I lift my gaze to see his flare with lust. I shake my head in silent response, flicking my tongue over my quivering lower lip.

Ballas stretches his arm out and reaches forward to depress the pad of his thumb in the middle of my lip. He pulls down, my jaw releasing and I open my mouth wide.

"I fantasized about this mouth on my cock while I got myself off in the shower."

The dirty image has me gasping as wetness floods my panties. My nipples pebble hard against my shirt, straining for his touch.

He slides his thumb along my lower lip from one corner of my mouth to the other.

"I'm going to give you one choice, princess. And after that, all the decisions are mine, do you understand?"

I nod in understanding. Everything about this erotically fun foreplay and the delicious sexual appeal of Ballas turns me on and this time, I don't want to stop.

"Good girl. You can either beg for forgiveness with words," he says, sliding two of his fingers in my mouth to press down on my tongue, "or use this mouth to make amends by sucking my cock down your throat. Which will it be? Choose wisely."

Ballas leans back against the couch cushion so casually you'd think he's just asked me if it will rain instead of whether I wanted to give him a blowjob. He drops his hand to his straining erection between his spread legs, his pants tented, and gives a leisurely stroke while his dark eyes remain glued on me.

I arch a brow, tilting my head in playful consideration.

"Both options have merit," I sigh with a coy grin. "Maybe you should choose for me."

The minute those words leave my mouth, his hands grab his waistband and he tugs his pants down to his knees. His cock strains upright, hard, and beautiful.

I drink him in, my fingers itching to touch him and my mouth filling with saliva in anticipation of what's to come. My pussy clenches at the thought of how good it will feel when his dick finally, *finally* slams inside.

This is happening. Tonight. Now.

I'm fascinated as Ballas wraps his fist tightly around his stiff dick and casually strokes it from base to tip. I let out a puff of disappointment which elicits a cheeky grin from him.

"Is there something you want, princess?" His tone is raspy now, teasingly dirty, but the expression on his face is mischievous, a single eyebrow arching with amusement.

"Do you want my cock, sweetheart?"

"Mmm-hmmm." I nod enthusiastically, generously licking my lips in preparation for his dick.

"Good girl. Then come here and suck it."

I waste no time, bending over his lap while his hand lands at the back of my head, grabbing onto my loose strands of hair. I open as wide as I can go, his hand guiding the head of his taut length between my lips. His cock slides over the flat of my tongue. My mouth is full of him. I drink in his scent and salty taste, then suck him in deep. When he hits the back of my throat and I moan around him, it draws out a long groan of satisfaction from his chest.

Using the flat of my tongue, I slide it up the steely length, teasing and playing as I go. His cock jerks in my mouth and I smile around the girth.

"That's right, princess. Keep smiling when my cock hits you deep."

His erection pulses inside my mouth, as if reaching for what it wants, as I hollow out my cheeks while sucking him back before sliding off and sucking around his perfect crown.

"Oh fuck yeah...faster now...take it...yeah... that's fucking perfect."

His words encourage me on, as does the rough hand that fists my hair for leverage, directing my movements. He grips my hair tight and tugs, sending ripples of heat directly to my sex. I work to breathe, sucking air through my nose in tiny sips, when his cockhead hits the back of my throat.

I hum around the base and roll back up as I can feel the tension rising in the flex of his tight abdomen. His thick thighs underneath my palms ripple with tension and his hips buck and strain upward as I swallow him down.

Tears form in the corners of my eyes from the intrusion. I like the way this feels and the way Ballas dominates this space in my head and dictates the rules of my body.

I'm carefree and able to let go with abandon when it's Ballas calling the shots.

Suddenly, Ballas wrenches free and yanks my head back, leaving my mouth empty and void of him. For a moment, I think he's pulling out so he doesn't come down my throat.

My eyes fly up to his as his chest heaves and his eyes burn with heat.

"I want to come inside your pussy. *Now*."

25

B allas

I hoist Karis up from her knees and carry her over to the pool table that I've had dirty thoughts about since I first saw it. I want her bent over like an offering while I fuck her from behind, her legs spread eagle and her arms above her head. She huffs out a giggle when I set her down on her feet in front of it and begin to remove her clothes.

She leans back with her palms on the green felt and peers behind her. "The pool table?"

I waggle my brows and nod, lifting her arms up to tug off her sweater exposing her supple breasts. I kiss along the slope of her collarbone as she arches her back and tips her head to offer me more. It's a lesson in patience as I silently study her naked body, relearning every curve with the glide of my calloused fingers. My demanding lips explore the satin of her skin, drawing a path from the plunge of her cleavage down to her belly.

"The minute I saw this table, I knew I'd be fucking you on it."

Her mouth quirks up at the corners. "Pretty sure of yourself."

I crash my mouth to hers, plunging my tongue between her lips as I wedge my hand between her legs. Dipping my finger between her folds, I flirt with the wetness there and then draw it up to her belly button, circling the wetness over her navel.

"I had a good idea this would happen sooner or later."

She moans when I gently push at her shoulders until she's flat against the table and then bend over her stomach to lick her essence away with the tip of my tongue.

She bucks her hips up. "Don't tease me, Ballas. We've waited long enough."

With a growl, I press my palm on the flat of her stomach.

"Bossy little princess, aren't you?" I return my fingers to her pussy and sink them into her tight, wet heat. We both groan in synchronicity.

The tension in my balls grows tight and it's possible I could snap like a rubber band if I don't get inside her quick. I take a hand and stroke it over my engorged cock, swirling my finger over the pre-cum gathered at the tip.

Karis squirms with pleasure when I glide my arousal over a stiff nipple, marking her with my seed. She gasps softly and the sound penetrates something deep inside me, unplugging the dam that is about to burst.

Another growl rumbles from my chest when she rolls her thumb over the nub and moans when she brings it to her mouth.

"Mmm."

That sound drives me to the edge, pushing me to losing all vestiges of my already straining control.

Tugging each leg with a grip around her ankles, I yank her ass to the edge of the table. Then with one large fist, I bind her wrists and lift them above her head. With my weeping cockhead nestled at her entrance, I hold myself above her and lean down to give her a blinding kiss.

It's tempting to thrust inside her wet folds, her body opening so willingly for me.

"I'm going to fuck this bossy pussy of yours," I croak in a low curse, sliding my cock once again through the excruciatingly wet heat. My arms shake at the raw pleasure of feeling the mixture of our arousals coating the length of my cock. I squeeze my eyes shut as we simultaneously moan together. "Fuck me, though. I don't have a condom."

I lose all sense of space and time with each slide of my cock, with each wild and passionate kiss, and with the need to be buried inside her.

I pin Karis in place by circling my hips, my cock wedged at her entrance.

The world stops turning, and time stands still when Karis spreads her legs wide, opening her body up to me.

"I don't want to wait," she pleads on a sexy moan. My fingers tighten their grip on her wrists. "I want to feel your cock inside."

I press the head of my cock into her wet entrance. "Are you sure?"

She digs her heels into the small of my back and she arches hers.

In one swift move, I thrust deep inside her.

Oh fuck. It's heaven.

My body reacts with eager anticipation as a fireball of sensation whips through my tightening balls and up my spine. Karis keens out a desperate cry.

I'm gone for this woman. Abso-fucking-lutely gone. And there's no going back now.

I begin to move in earnest, grunting with each thrust. Our hands lock together, fingers gripping tightly as we climb together toward our individual pleasures.

When my eyes meet hers and I see the intensity there, it's as if I'm looking directly into her soul. I blink at the honesty bared in those green eyes. It's almost too much.

I pull out and flip her over onto her belly, grasping her hips in my rough fingers to slam back inside.

"Hold on tight," I encourage, rocking my rigid shaft at an angle that leaves me blurry-eyed.

Karis's body trembles when I zero in on her clit, pressing my fingers over her sensitive nub and stroking her with every thrust. This position allows me to both feel her deep and block out the raw emotion in her expression.

I stroke her swollen flesh, her moans growing with a sense of urgency.

"Are you going to come for me, princess?"

Karis rears back, her inner walls clenching around my shaft. My restraint diminishes as her wet, satin heat urges me closer to that precipice, my balls demanding release.

"Ballas...I'm there....so close."

Slipping my other hand to her tits, I squeeze her firm breast, plumping the round flesh as she arches into my hand. The moment I pinch her nipple, her body quivers. Her breath hitches as my dick hits a spot deep within her walls. She drops her head between her shoulders, trembling out her orgasm with a whimper of pleasure.

"That's a good girl," I murmur against her ear, my body bowing over hers. "Your orgasm is mine. It belongs to me."

I continue to circle her swollen clit until her body relaxes, muscles loosening as she practically falls limp. I wrap my arm around her waist, slamming inside until I feel the start of my own orgasm as it spirals down my back, my thighs tensing and everything inside of me swirling in a victory dance.

With a savage snarl, I bellow out my release and grab the base of my shaft to pull out from her tight heat. I throw my head back in rapturous ecstasy, shuttering with the eruption as I come hotly over her back. The thick spirals of my release cover the track of her scar along her spine, molding the pain of her past to mix with the aftershocks of my pleasure.

I slowly come back to reality and an unusual sense of discomfort settles in my chest, an uneasiness like I've never had before.

I reach for the shirt I discarded in a heap and use it to away the remnants of my climax painted her back.

"Are you okay?"

Karis flips over to sit up with a contented smirk leaving me with no doubt of her satisfaction.

"I think I'm more than okay." Her face glows with post-coital endorphins and her smile clears away all the doubts that jumbled in my head. I'm only filled with a sense of pride for making this beautiful woman feel the way she does now.

"Glad to know I did my job."

She stands upright and stretches her arms toward the ceiling. The sleek curve of her body entices me to take her back into the bedroom for another round.

"Goddamn, you are one fucking sexy woman," I murmur, gently stroking a hand over her naked body.

I gather her into my arms and with slow caresses, I trace the generous curves, the dips and valleys, running my fingers over her soft skin. She closes her eyes with a soft sigh.

I lead down close and press my lips to the dip in her neck, breathing in her scent.

"You do know what they say about hockey players, don't you?"

My tongue laps at her skin, tracing over the flesh along her shoulder and up her neck until I reach her earlobe, clasping it between my teeth. I tug at it and she inhales sharply.

Her voice comes out in a rasp. "That they're cocky?"

"Ha! True, but not what I meant."

I hum against her neck while my hand glides over the curve of her hips. There I fit my palm under the round curve of her butt and swing her legs into my arms and head down the hallway toward the guestroom.

"Ballas," she says with a hint of disapproval. "You shouldn't exert yourself. We're already pushing it with protocol."

I snort at her misguided concern and drop her on the bed in a naked, beautiful heap, I continue to nibble and suck all the exposed sensual skin. I rest my body on top of her, nestling my leg and cock into the V of her legs so she can feel my already growing erection.

"We hockey players are capable of extremely high levels of endurance and profound stamina."

"Oh yeah?"

"Which means I'm ready to go again."

She lifts her head to stare down at my very hard erection between us, then takes it in her grip, stroking it roughly, pulling out a long grunt from my chest. She throws a leg over my hip to open her entrance as I slip two fingers inside, feeling her still wet and ready. I grind against her pelvis in an erotic rhythm.

"Don't pull out," she demands boldly. "I want you to feel you lose yourself inside me."

Oh hell yeah.

I've never fucked bare.

But with Karis, we share a level of trust that goes beyond the hockey connection.

Maybe it's because Karis doesn't want anything from me—not my fame, not my money, not even my name. She already has that for herself in spades. For all intents and purposes, she already owns me in every sense of the word.

She owns me.

The thought sinks into my brain with what little blood supply is there and ricochets back down to my cock.

"Are you sure this is okay with you?" My cock jerks at her entrance, so ready to tunnel back inside her pussy.

"Yes," she whispers. "I'm protected and so are you."

My balls ache and my cock throbs as I thrust into her tight channel and give her everything she's asked for.

"You're the boss."

26

K aris

Ballas is dangerous.

He's a menace to my senses, a threat to my logic and a certain danger to my heart.

There's a very different reason why he's called The Beast. This man will devour me like a predator does its prey.

From day one, he's unearthed a woman in me I never knew existed, a daring part of me that is insatiable and wants more, more, *more*.

Ballas fucked me several more times last night and once again this morning against the cold hard shower tiles. He coaxed my body into one mind-blowing orgasm after another, leaving boneless and limp until I could barely walk straight.

Afterwards, he goes back to sleep and I finish getting ready to head into the office, the soreness between my legs a reminder of just how thoroughly it was used.

As I often do in the morning, I watch all the latest sporting news and listen to the reports as I put on my makeup and do my hair, interested in the latest commentary about the teams and players in both the leagues.

One in particular has me dropping my makeup wand on the floor, my body stiffening when I hear the name.

"We all know that Toronto player, Sergei Russo, who has been suspended due to an illegal hit against Vikings defensemen, Ballas Keeney, is now facing charges for alleged assault against an unnamed woman."

My jaw drops. What in the ever-loving…?

The TV broadcaster continues. "Apparently, it was after the news of his suspension yesterday that Russo allegedly went on a bender and became violent with a woman he was with that night."

"I've seen how Russo plays," breaks in the other broadcaster. "It's a shame they don't know where the violence needs to end when they step off the ice and into the real world. Isn't that also the case with Pilots' center, Hammond Greis?"

"It's true that both men have been charged with alleged battery, but we don't know the full facts yet with Russo. We'll have to wait to see how the cases against them turn out. In the meantime, Russo has a lot more to contend with than his long-standing rivalry with Keeney."

"Speaking of Ballas Keeney, we heard from sources close to the team today that while on the injured reserve for an upper-body injury, Keeney may be put on waivers from the Vikings, which could even mean he's off the ice permanently…"

"That's right, John. Vikings' GM Nate McGowan has said they've recalled AHL D-man, Chris Stolley and the source insists he may be taking Ballas's spot for good."

My blood turns to ice. *Nate.* That motherfucking cocksucker.

I twist my neck to stare in flat-out horror at the television, blindly reaching for my phone to dial up my GM. It goes to voicemail. I'm sure he knows exactly what I'm calling about and is just trying to avoid me. Well, his cowardly tactics won't last too long because I'm about to lay into him.

I leave a message once I hear the beep, the tone of my voice cold, which is exactly how I feel toward him right now.

It's as if he wants to give me more reason to fire his ass.

"Nate, it's Karis. I will be in the office by…" I trail off, checking the time. "Nine a.m. You will be there waiting for me to discuss final decisions about our roster."

I hang up without saying goodbye and finish getting ready. My body is a livewire, amped and lit up with so much anger I could spit nails. That is until I peek in the guest room and find Ballas sleeping soundly, arms laced behind his head, snoring lightly.

The tension in my body eases as tingles of sexual energy take the place of my irritation. I wish I could just remain home to watch him sleep, his dark eyelashes fanning out as if trying to reach his cheekbones.

Ballas exudes sex appeal even in his sleep. How is that even possible? Perhaps it's his physical prowess along with his strength or the way he takes control to ensure I'm completely satisfied before he takes his own pleasure.

After our sexcapades last night, I'm not sure how I'll hide my longing toward Ballas when we're together. It'll be written all over my face the minute someone mentions his name. Even now, my body comes alive the moment I'm confronted with his presence—the invisible pheromones splicing through the air to mingle and dance with mine, turning me into a hot mess of hormones.

I inhale deeply and close my eyes, reminding myself this isn't permanent. When I return home tonight, Ballas will be gone and it will feel like none of this ever happened. It can't happen again. Can it?

Suddenly, a hand darts out and ensnares my wrist. A startled screech escapes my lungs as my eyes fly open to find Ballas awake and staring hungrily at me. With one quick tug, I'm pulled off my feet and land on top of him.

I fall in a tangle of limbs over his warm body, enveloped in his deliciously masculine, musky scent, his muscular arms hooked around my waist.

"Were you just staring at me like a creeper?"

"*W*-what? No...I wasn't."

Ballas chuckles at my bold lie and somehow manages to flip me over onto my back to pin me underneath his nearly naked body. With one hand, he locks my wrists together above my head and wedges a leg between my thighs. And like a ninja, he rucks up my skirt above my knees. The soft bristle of the fine hair of his legs teases at my inner thighs and the heat of his thick length presses against the silk of my panties.

The panties that are already soaked with my own arousal.

"Have I told you how hard I get when I see you dressed like a badass boss?"

His fingers snag the hem of my blouse that had just been neatly tucked into the waistband of my skirt. He tugs it out with the dexterity of a superhero, undoing all the buttons to expose my white lace bra underneath.

"Ballas...I have to go..." My words die on my lips the moment he begins peppering my stomach with kisses. The scrape of his beard as he makes his way up to my breast is a delicious reason to cancel all my plans for the day.

He yanks the cups of my bra down and sucks a puckered nipple between his teeth, laving his tongue over the stiff peak.

It's beautiful torture. I whimper and clutch at the back of his head with my free hand to keep him there and demand more.

"You looked stressed," he murmurs, the sound muffled as he drags his lips over the valley of my breasts to pamper the other one. His mouth latches on as he nibbles and then scrapes his teeth over my taut nipple. "You can't start your day stressed out. Plus, the doctor said I need to increase my stamina. I figure I can kill two birds with one stone."

I giggle. "Oh, it's as hard as stone, that's for sure."

"Damn right it is. All for you."

With one swift motion, his cock is freed and he slips a hand between my legs to tug my panties to the side. My body shifts forward as he slams inside, burying himself to the hilt.

"Oh fuck, princess," he exclaims breathlessly, his hard length filling me completely. My inner walls spasm and clench around his steely heat. "Why does it feel better every fucking time?"

The incredulous tone in his question expresses the very same thoughts I've had each time we've been together. I'm insatiable for him and can't get enough. He's my own personal brand of Skittles. I can never get my fill.

"I don't know...I just want more of you."

His body undulates over me and my gaze lifts to watch the ripples of his abs move and flex with each thrust.

My breasts bounce as he slams into me. Each time he bottoms out, he gyrates his hips, his pelvis rubbing my clit until I'm screaming out his name like a prayer.

"Oh, Ballas...yes...there...right there."

As if I just gave him the permission needed, Ballas stills on top of me and roars out a string of curses, chasing his own orgasm that barrels through him.

Collapsing on top of me, his face lolls to the side of my neck. His warm breath fans against my ear as his chest rises and falls in slowing rhythm.

After a few minutes, I feel the essence of him trickling down my leg and I know I need to clean myself up before I leave.

Ballas lifts his head from the crook in my neck and his words make me smile.

"Did I just fuck the stress out of you or was that a dream?"

Pressing his palms near my shoulders, he pushes himself up to hover over me, his cock sliding out of my body. I wince at the barren feeling his absence leaves behind.

"I suppose you wouldn't consider staying like this?" He drags a finger through the wetness seeping from between my legs, and I suck in a shaky breath. "I would be hard all day knowing I left a part of me painted on your thighs while you did all the bossy things."

He steals my response with a blazing hot kiss and I actually consider his request.

Because truthfully, it would be the hottest thing ever.

27

K aris

In the end, I did do a slight quick cleanup, as well as retouch my lipstick and brush through my hair before I left for the office. I still made it in plenty of time before my scheduled meeting with Nate.

I did, however, leave a trace of Ballas on my upper thigh. It felt naughty and dangerous and I need all of that as I now peruse Nate's file, reading through the notes left in the margins in Marv's messy handwritten script.

A wave of homesick despair hits me hard, but I swallow it back.

I will not let myself succumb to sadness and stress. Not right now, not when I need to keep my chin up and head held high and maintain a level of composure to get through this meeting.

Thank God Ballas did what he promised. The quickie this morning alleviated my stress and calmed my nerves, leaving me ready to have a rational, fact-based discussion with Nate. Had I gone into this meeting without Ballas's very helpful intervention, I may have been an emotional mess, which would have given Nate more reason to be a disrespectful dick to me.

Who am I kidding? Nate's always like that with me and this conversation is gearing up to be an ugly mess. I can't expect him to act like a professional when he's never proven he is one.

On my way in this morning, I called the Tarjinder, and asked him to be here to consult on my plans and the points I want to cover before Nate arrives.

Tar now sits in one of my office guest chairs and reviews Nate's contract.

"Obviously, Karis, you have the right to terminate his contract at any time for any reason, assuming you pay out the terms of the agreement." He flips through the pages of the contract on his iPad, glasses perched on the tip of his nose as he reads through the fine print. When he lifts his gaze, I feel a sense of a relief in his dark and sure eyes. "I think it's good that you're doing this earlier rather than later in the season. It will allow you to find someone who can jump in before we get too far in the weeds. It's also the last year in his contract, giving Nate his payout and time to find something else."

His vote of confidence reassures me and fills me with some relief from my panic. Tar's next question, however, gives me a case of heartburn, like I just ate a Taco Bell burrito at midnight.

"Have you run through a list of prospective replacements yet? We will need to get the word out immediately to those on your short list. Do you have someone in mind?"

I stand from my desk and begin pacing, counting my steps forward before spinning around and counting them back again.

Tar waits expectantly for my response, sitting with one leg crossed over his knee, hands in his lap in a dignified pose.

"I have been looking at a few. Obviously, we need to conduct a search and narrow it down quickly. There's also a possibility of an internal candidate," I hedge, dropping my chin and glancing at him through my eyelashes. It makes me nervous to even say the name out loud because of where things currently stand with Ballas. He didn't express interest when I hinted at the possibility.

Besides, he's still going to play this year, which means I'd still have to find someone else as a temporary fill-in.

"Oh?" he says. His brows pinch together. "Who is that?"

I swallow down my nerves and am about to say Ballas's name when there's a knock on the door and Christine pops her head through the crack.

"Nate's here to see you, Karis. Would you all like something to drink?"

I smile at my assistant and nod. "Yes, please. Water is fine."

She swings the door open, moving out of the way to allow Nate to come in. He barrels through, practically stepping on Christine's shoes, and stops short with a deep scowl the moment he notices Tar.

"What's this about? Why is he here?" Nate's voice is hard as he nods toward Tarjinder, killing any potential empathy I've tried to retain for my soon-to-be-former GM. Tar keeps his unblinking gaze on Nate and nods.

I slide one trembling hand in my pants pocket and signal to the open chair with the other.

"Please, have a seat, Nate."

He capitulates with an aggressive step to the chair, then sits down and crosses his arms defensively.

I swear, working with this man has been like dealing with an eight-year-old spoiled child. He's never been accommodating or willing to bend. He's rigid, inflexible, and unwilling to work with a woman.

And don't get me started on how he treats people that he sees as beneath him. I've witnessed his interactions with our staff and the toxicity that exudes from his behavior. That's not the type of environment I want in our head offices. Or for my team.

My team.

This is the first time since taking over for Marv that I've actually felt like it is my team.

I sit down and straighten my shoulders, using every bit of height and stature I can muster to make my appearance bigger than it is. Both Tarjinder's and my height pale in comparison to Nate's imposingly tall frame.

"I watched the sports news this morning." I let that sink in and wait for Nate to put the pieces together.

His jaw tics. "So? Don't we all?"

I lean forward and place my forearms on the desk, clasping my hands together. Mostly to keep them from shaking.

"Somehow there were details about Stolley and Keeney and plans for the team," I say, pinning him with a stare, "that no one else should have been privy to. Discussions we've only had privately. You and me." I gesture between us with my index finger.

Nate bristles and squirms in his chair, looking a little less composed now under my scrutiny. "It's all conjecture. You know those journalists; they make shit up for ratings."

"You were quoted, Nate. As in, the source." I use air quotes, shaking my head in disappointment.

"That's bullshit, Karis. You know it."

I push back in my chair and stand. I want to have the height advantage as I proceed with the final blow.

"Nate, I'm letting you go, effective immediately."

With a loud roar, Nate stands, leans forward and slams a fist on my desk.

"You can't fucking do this, you bitch! I'm under contract through the end of this season."

I flinch at the term and violent outburst and take a step back. My gaze flicks to Tarjinder, who stands and moves to the side of my desk in a protective reminder to Nate not to do anything stupid.

"Nate," he says in a calm voice. "You've been in this league long enough to know these contracts are terminable by either party at any time for any reason. You will be paid out under the remaining terms of the agreement, assuming you…"

"Fucking bullshit! If your uncle wasn't a goddamn vegetable right now, this wouldn't be happening," Nate fumes, pointing an accusatory finger at me, his expression dark and menacing. "You have no idea what you're doing. You're just a fucking little rich girl playing grownup with your uncle's team. You're a laughing stock of everyone in the NHL. You'll never play with the big boys."

In the past, I would've cowered at his vitriol and hurtful words. I would have burst into tears at hearing no one liked me and that I wasn't good enough to be here.

Despite the severe sting his remarks cause and the trembling of my knees, I manage to keep my tone composed and my response professional. I will not get into it with this man who I've barely tolerated the last six months. Good riddance.

"I understand you're upset, Nate. You have a right to feel the way you do. But you don't have the right to hurl insults or use derogatory language about me or Marvin." I turn to pick up the form Tarjinder printed out earlier and hand it to Nate. He glares down at my hand as if he wants to slap it away, glowering before snapping the paper from my fingers. "Here is your contract release. HR is waiting down in your office and will escort you out. We will have all your things packed up and sent to you at your address on file. I wish you well and thank you for time with the Vikings."

With a snarl and a murderous glare, Nate spins around and stomps toward the door, swinging it open with such force it bangs against the wall.

"You have no idea what you're doing to this team, Karis," he says over his shoulder. "You just fucked yourself and the team in the ass with this decision. You'll be hearing from my attorney soon."

When he's cleared the hallway of my office, I finally let out the breath I'd been holding in. Tar pats my hand that I had in a white-knuckled grip on the edge of my desk.

"It went as good as can be expected. You did wonderfully, Karis."

I wring my hands together nervously, replaying everything that was said and the horrible comments Nate made. "Thank you, Tar. I just hope I made the right decision."

Gathering up his things, he smiles at me. "In all honesty, it probably should have been done long before this. I think Marvin was just an optimist and held out hope Nate would come around to the organization's values."

Tar's comments mean more to me than anything ever could.

Sometimes we hang on to things far longer than we should.

A valuable lesson to learn in both business and in life.

28

B allas

It feels good to be back in the training room, even though I'm only doing a light workout to warm up and keep my body agile.

Although, truth be told, my body already went through a warmup this morning when I fucked Karis before she left for the office.

Goddamn, what a way to start the morning.

Our team's assistant trainer, Beau Gather, remained behind while the team is on the road trip and now gives me a weird look over the top of his clipboard. "What the fuck you smiling about, Keeney? You think I'm going to go easy on you just because you hit your pretty head?"

I snort, knocking on my temple with my knuckles. "This head has taken a lot of hard knocks. No problem there. I'm ready to go."

"Good. Now give me fifteen deep squats." He circles his clipboard toward the matted floor of the training room. I nod and do as he says.

After that, Beau has me doing stop-and-go push-ups, then single-leg T-stands on both legs, and then right into push-ups. By the time our junior equipment manager Jeremy—dubbed as The Beav because he's so damn innocent—walks in, I have sweat dripping down my back and I'm a bit winded and dizzy.

Fuck. That's not good.

Beau pushes me to the point of fatigue. "Come on, Keeney. Now some dive bombers."

I'm still on the floor, ready to maneuver into the pendulum-like move, when Jeremy bursts like a dam with his news.

"Holy smokes did you guys hear?" he asks breathlessly, practically bouncing on his feet, a stack of towels in his arms.

Thankful for the interruption, I pause my repetitions and look over at him, hoping that the news has nothing to do with another player injury. That's the last thing we need so early in the season.

"Hear what?" I ask, pushing myself up to sit with my legs stretched out in front of me. I bend over and reach to touch my toes to keep myself limbered up. I let out a low groan of displeasure.

Fuck, I'm feeling my age. The head is doing much better but doesn't help in matters much, either.

Beav leans in and whispers conspiratorially, scanning

around as if on some sort of secret mission. "McGowan got canned!"

"What?"

"When?" I chime in over Beau's question. We both stare at Beav in disbelief.

Beav nods his head furiously as a wide grin plays across his baby face.

"Just now…someone saw him storming out of Ms. Spurlock's office followed by the Director of HR, then he was escorted from the building by security minutes later." He takes a big breath. "He looked pissed as hell."

I furrow my brows and recall Karis's question about what I thought of Nate. Surely that wasn't the reason he got fired. Karis uses facts and data to make her decisions so I know it wasn't because I called him an asshat.

Beau hums politely, adding nothing more.

"Interesting. Thanks for the info, Beav. I'm sure we'll be hearing from Karis soon."

"No problem, Keeney. Anything for you. See you guys later."

Beav scurries off to replenish the stock of towels in the locker room while Beau checks his phone.

"There's nothing in the news yet and no company-wide email in my inbox." He turns his attention to me as I continue my stretches to keep my body from cooling down too much. "Between you and me, I say good fucking riddance if it's true. McGowan was a nutsack."

I snicker. "And that's being generous."

Beau nudges my thigh with the toe of his sneaker. "Let me remind you, I'm not a nice person. Now get back to it, Keeney. Give me fifteen more and then we're starting it all again."

I groan loudly but capitulate. In the long run, this will help me avoid losing too much agility and strength while I continue my recovery.

Just as I finish a twenty-minute run on the treadmill, dripping with sweat and probably smelling like days-old trash, Karis steps through the glass double-doors of the team workout room.

I wipe at my forehead with a towel. Beau is standing behind me and can't see me as I take a long, slow scan up her body, my gaze stopping at the hem of her skirt. She looks fresh and beautiful.

And I want to sully her up like I did earlier today.

Her long, blonde hair is now pulled away from her face into a sleek ponytail. I grab the machine handles to keep myself from automatically reaching out to cup her cheeks and plant a hot kiss on her lips.

Beau smiles in greeting, completely unaware of the sexual tension between Karis and me. "Good morning, Ms. Spurlock. Can I help you with something?"

His tone makes it glaringly obvious that this is the first time she's ever come down for a visit. The thought makes me want to howl *this woman is mine*.

"Hello, Beau. Good morning." Her gaze leaves him and searches me out next to the machine. Karis locks eyes with mine and she clears her throat with a short cough. "I'm here to see Ballas."

I raise my brows and shrug. Then I look down at my attire.

"Uh, do you mind if I clean up quick?"

Did she just lick her lips or is that wishful thinking?

My thoughts go back to this morning when I dissuaded her from cleaning up after I fucked her hard and fast. The fact that she left the apartment with a part of me still left on the inside of her thighs has me wanting to crow like the cocky bastard I am.

She considers my request and looks down at her watch. "That's fine. Can you meet me in my office in ten minutes?"

I throw the towel over my shoulder and nod. "That works."

When she strides out the door, Beau coughs into his fist, giving me a look that says, *I hope you come back in one piece.*

"Same time tomorrow?" I ask, whistling as I head toward the locker room to get showered and changed. My thoughts are already working out the reason Karis wants to see me in private in her office.

"Yeah. Good luck with that," he replies, hooking a thumb in the direction Karis went. "Let's hope she's not a firing rampage this week."

I chuckle and walk into the showers, being as quick and efficient as I can before I head up to the office floor of the practice facility.

The elevator door swings open with a soft *bing* and I step off, turning the corner to walk down the hallway toward Karis's office. Christine's head pops up as she hears my approach and she smiles brightly from behind her desk.

"Hey Ballas. How's the noggin?" She raps her knuckles on her own head as I did earlier with Beau.

"I'm still dumb but lucky as fuck," I say with a self-deprecating laugh. "Nothing much has changed there."

Christine giggles and stands, leading the way into Karis's office. When the door opens, I'm gifted with the view of Karis behind her desk, staring at her laptop. When she lifts her head and smiles, those green eyes full of appreciation and offer a kaleidoscope of intelligence and confidence.

Karis extends an arm out in front of her. "Have a seat, Ballas. There's something I need to discuss with you."

K aris

Christine shuts the door, leaving me alone with Ballas. He offers me a sexy smirk and takes a seat, his gaze never leaving mine. In it I read what he's thinking.

He probably believes I've called him up here to have a secret rendezvous and to see him again because I can't stay away from him.

While that's partially the truth, the business reason I've invited him up overrides those personal desires, the ones I should've left in the bedsheets when I came to work this morning.

Ballas's eyes roam over my face. "You wanted to see me?" Now that we're alone in my office, he drops the veneer. "Is this about Nate?"

My eyes narrow. "How do you know about that?"

"I don't exactly." He shrugs and the material of his T-shirt tightens noticeably around his bulging biceps. "Rumors are swirling that he was fired."

Okay, here goes. I heave out a breath but dip into my candy dish to grab some reinforcements. It's been a struggle all morning and I've vacillated a number of times on how to approach this correctly with Ballas. I just need to blurt it out and see how he reacts to my proposal.

"Right...well, they are true. Nate is no longer our team GM."

Ballas smiles broadly and pumps a fist in the air in animated celebration. He reaches his arm forward and presents me with his fist and we bump our knuckled hands together. At least he's happy about that. Let's hope I don't douse the excitement with the secondary topic of discussion.

"I really want to kiss you right now." He swings his head to glance over his shoulder and then back to me, his voice lowering to a secret hush. "But that will have to wait 'til tonight."

"Ballas," I say, my voice tremoring slightly. "I've made some decisions about the management of the organization and they affect you."

He sits back in his chair, his enthusiasm diminishing and morphing into uncertain curiosity.

"I want to end your players contract—"

He doesn't let me finish. "What the actual fuck, Karis? Why the hell would you do that?" I bristle at his derisive tone and the anger flashing in his eyes.

I slide forward to the edge of my chair, leaning in toward Ballas who is quietly seething.

"Please, hear me out. Let me start over so I don't botch this up any further." He sits back with some reluctance, folding his arms across his chest. I inhale and try again. "I know you love playing hockey and you're under contract. But you're at a crossroads right now physically. Do you really want to return to the ice with the possibility that *one more hit* could end things for you completely? That your retirement wouldn't be on your terms?"

He rises to his feet and he strides over to the bank of windows, the broad set of his shoulders rising and falling with shallow breaths and a heavy awkward silence descends over us.

Shit. I knew this would be difficult for him to get his head wrapped around. I'd hoped he'd listen to my offer and realize my intentions come from a good place. A place in my heart that cares about him so much more than just a player.

I continue. "Ballas, the offer I want you to consider takes into account the needs of the team and your continued success in the league. Just in a different capacity. I want you to stay with the team."

He remains with his back to me when he finally speaks, words sharp like knives. "You can't make this decision for me. It's my choice, Karis. Not yours. I will end my career when I say it's over and how I see fit."

Oh, this man. This stubborn, beautiful man.

I cross the room to face him. We're inches from one another and I can smell the spicy, soapy scent of his soap, but he might as well be miles away. He keeps his gaze averted and avoids looking at me, his arms crossed defiantly over his chest.

Clasping my hands in front of me, I consider my next words carefully.

"I see so much leadership potential in you, Ballas. I don't want to lose you." I pause and catch my breath. "But I want you to stay in the role of the general manager. I want you to replace Nate."

A loud burst of wry laughter barrels from his chest. "You can't be serious, Karis. I'm not made to sit in an office, to push paperclips and host lunch meetings." He crooks his fingers and then pins me with his stormy eyes. "I'm an athlete. I don't know shit all about managing a hockey team. I make plays out on the ice, not in a fucking boardroom."

"But for how long?" It comes out as barely a whisper but conveys my deep-rooted concern over Ballas's health and his ability to play long-term.

He snarls, baring his teeth in a mocking grin. "I'm not in a fucking retirement home wearing adult diapers quite yet, princess."

Twisting away from me and back to the window. When I find my voice again, I clasp a hand around his thick forearm and tug at him to look at me.

"It's never too late to reinvent yourself, Ballas." I cup his scruffy face in my hands, the stubble of his beard scratching my palms. Our eyes lock and I see a flash of something unreadable flittering in his gaze. "Either way, you'll be retiring soon. And then what? I'm offering you the opportunity to start a new career in a leadership role before you're forty. Why wait and risk getting really injured? This is a great chance to start that new chapter in your career now and under your own terms."

He stares down at me for what feels like an eternity.

"You mean, under *your* terms," he sneers, shaking my hands free. "Let's not forget, you're the boss."

I let him go and step back over to my desk where I plunge my hand inside my candy dish again, scooping out a handful of Skittles. I toss them in my mouth one by one, counting down to regain some composure.

I heave a sigh of heaviness in my chest. "It's not about me, but what's best for the team and for you."

Ballas whips around. "Because you think I'm not capable and I'm too old to play. Well, fuck that. I'm still in prime shape and can outplay and outskate any motherfucking guy out there. I don't need you—a spoiled twenty-something princess who will probably be bored of this job before the season's out—giving me career advice."

The pain of those words slices through my heart. I know he's upset and I shouldn't take it personally but damn, that hurts.

Ballas turns on his heels and heads to the door. Before he leaves, though, he turns to look at me over his shoulder, hurling another one I never saw coming.

"You can take me out of your potential candidate list and go fuck the next guy on your shortlist. We're done here."

And just like that, the man who told me I could trust him and who would have my back has let me down and let his pride get in the way.

It's clear that I'm just another meaningless hookup on Ballas's long list of conquests. And I'm the fool who believed I was something else.

30

B allas

"Come on, Keeners. Drink up, man. We've got to celebrate tonight," Dane Axelrod coaxes from the bar seat next to me, sliding another beer my way.

I think it's my third. No wait, fourth? Okay, maybe it's the fifth drink we've downed tonight and I'm just feeling like a goddamn lightweight. The effects of the booze have me woozy and have already given me the spins. "Here's to your return to the game, another win, and an official adios to that fuckhead, McGowan!"

I clink my glass to his without looking up. Instead, I stare down at the cocktail napkin in front of me—like the one I used to create an origami gift to Karis—and I grumble like the broody bastard I am. Except I can't seem to focus my vision and the bartop won't stop squirming.

Am I drunk?

Ax gives up on me when a woman taps him on the shoulder and he spins around to give her his trademark smile at the prospect. I keep my head hung low and listen as he chats up the puck bunny.

He's right about one thing. Instead of being a sullen, drunken bastard, I should be celebrating my fucking stellar return. My restrictions were lifted this week after a full fourteen-days off the ice, getting me back on the roster just in time to help the team win at home tonight.

Even my two assists and our two points don't seem enough to lift my surly mood. Nothing does since I stormed out of Karis's office three weeks ago like the fucking idiot I am.

It came as one hell of a surprise when Coach Thomas gave me the green light and put me back in the starting line-up tonight. Part of me figured Karis had the right to seek some bossy revenge and keep me out for how disrespectfully I treated her during our conversation.

But deep inside, I know Karis that isn't how she plays. She plays fair and doesn't hold grudges. I've seen her in action. I know how hard she works despite never wanting ownership of the Vikings in the first place. She makes solid business decisions in Marvin's absence and clearly puts the team's success first.

There is no one else out there who I've seen make more personal and professional sacrifices for this organization. I think her uncle would be damned proud of her for the way she's handled this transition.

You should tell her that, asshole.

Goddamn, I am ashamed of how poorly I responded when she suggested that I should hang up my skates before my contract ends, but it felt like a giant blow to my ego. She might as well had said I'm past my prime and not worth the risk.

After stewing over it for the past week, I realize I was just too scared to admit I may be overdue for retirement. My body is sure as shit shouting that message loud and clear right now after the beating I took out there tonight. I'm a coward for not seeing my reality clearly enough.

Karis, on the other hand, is the bravest woman I know. There is no one else who at twenty-nine could've stepped in and assume a role as big as the Vikings, along with her NBA team, and take it on with such grace and poise.

Thinking back now, I'm pretty sure I fell for Karis last Christmas Eve, the night I rushed to her side when Marv was admitted to the hospital.

The strength she possesses in one finger would put even the biggest and baddest D-man to shame. It definitely does me.

A nudge at my side knocks me off balance and I rock in my barstool. My vision swims with a blurry haze when I spin around to face Ax.

"Hey, Keeney. This here is Maya. She wants to know if we want to come back to her table where you can meet her friend, Winnie." Ax winks, downing his glass and hoisting it in the air as a request to the bartender for another one.

I may be drunk but I can already tell these women are far too young for me. Besides, they aren't Karis.

"Nah, I'm good. You three have fun. I'm calling it a night."

As soon as I stand, the floor drops out from under my feet and the world seems to tip on its side. I reach for something to grab on to, anything in the vicinity to keep me upright, but I miss the edge of the counter and my fingers fumble with the barstool. The stool, however, isn't strong enough to hold my 205-pound frame.

I slip and go toppling sideways.

Fortunately, Ax's quick reflexes save me when he hooks a hand in the crook of my elbow and pulls me upright.

"Whoa, man. Slow your roll. You good?" He pats me on the shoulder when I nod.

"Yeah, all good. Thanks, Ax."

Ax gives me an odd look as if I've just spoken a foreign language. I'm about to ask what's up when the light from the bar suddenly dims and the black-and-white checkered floor is the last thing I see as it comes flying to meet my face.

$\sim$

JUST EXACTLY HOW drunk am I?

Jesus, I don't remember drinking that much.

Why is there a flashing strobe light in my eyes?

Where the hell am I?

What's covering my nose and mouth?

I blindly lift my hand to my face and find an oxygen mask attached to my head. My eyes spring open and although they are slow to track, I take in the tubes and equipment and realize I'm in the back of an ambulance.

A latex-gloved hand covers mine gently. "Please keep that on for a bit longer, Mr. Keeney. Until your oxygen is back up to at least ninety, we need to keep this on."

"Did I pass out?" It feels like there's cotton in my mouth.

The young male EMT nods. "You took a doozy of a spill. Got an ugly goose egg on that head of yours, too. And your nose was a gusher. We finally got that stopped with a cotton roll under your lip."

Ahh. So, there *is* cotton in my mouth.

I try to piece together everything leading up to this moment but don't remember too much of it. That can't be a good sign.

Maybe it has something to do with the collision I had on the ice tonight when I slammed into the Boston player as we battled for possession of the puck. I'd checked him with my shoulder and his stick got stuck in my skate blade and I careened forward. Because we were at the glass, I hit my helmet hard against it, sending my head snapping back sharply.

Under normal circumstances, it's nothing to worry about. However, due to my recent concussion, I was immediately evaluated on the bench, taking me out for the remainder of the third period. I felt fine at the time. No blurry vision. No memory loss. Not even a headache.

But damn, now I'm not so sure it wasn't a secondary concussion. Obviously, it wasn't the beer that had me passing out at the bar.

I notice Ax standing outside the truck, talking animatedly

on his phone and staring at me with wary eyes. I narrow my eyebrows into a *what the fuck you doing* scowl.

He notices me watching him and nods, quickly putting an end to the call and walking toward me sheepishly.

"How you feeling, lightweight?" He chuckles, but something in his eyes tells me none of this is funny. I know what's going to happen next without so much as a word.

I know the score.

"Who was on the phone, Ax?" I ask brusquely, tugging the mask away from my nose and mouth to give him a menacing look.

Ax's eyes avoid me as he shrugs. When he returns my gaze, there's apology in his expression.

"I'm sorry, man, but I had to call Coach. It's for your own good. You didn't see how bad you looked." He blinks and looks toward the ground, giving his head a shake. "You went down hard."

I let my teammate off the hook, reaching for his hand to fist bump. "It's okay, man. You did me a solid. I would've done the same if I were in your situation."

"Thanks. It just—well, when you collapsed, Keeney, it freaked me the fuck out. I thought you were dead. I'm glad you aren't and the EMT says you're okay and don't have to go to the hospital." Then he leans in for emphasis, poking a finger in my thigh. "But you cost me a hookup tonight. You owe me."

I laugh at the young kid.

"You're not exactly my type," I joke. Then I notice the murderous glare I'm receiving from the EMT and snap the mask back over my mouth. Ax laughs and sucks in his bottom lip.

"No offense, but I'm not into you either, bro. But next time we hang after a game, you can't be pulling these stunts to be the center of attention and scaring off the puck bunnies. You feel me?"

My phone starts blowing up from inside my pocket before I can answer. I wiggle onto my side to pull it out and check the ID.

Damn, Coach Thomas.

I lift my brows and wave the phone at the EMT, who concedes with a resigned sigh.

I give a salute of appreciation and answer the call. "Hey, Coach. I suppose you've heard? Yeah, I'm fine. Nothing to worry about."

"Keeney, you're on speaker. I have Jerry from PR and Karis on the line with me."

I groan over the ambush and flop back against the uncomfortable gurney mattress.

"Hey, everyone. As you can hear, I'm fine."

"You're fine because you're a lucky son of a bitch," Coach grumbles. "This is not your first rodeo and these hits obviously haven't knocked any sense into you. Which is why we are putting you back on the IR list for the next four weeks."

"Fuck," I shout loudly, drawing the attention of the poor

EMT dude who startles in the confined space. I mouth, "Sorry," and close my eyes, trying to calm my frustration.

"Ballas, it's Jerry. We're drafting the press release to say it's an upper body injury with a week-to-week evaluation. The only thing you'll be doing, my friend, is getting some rest. No ice time. No workouts. No games."

It's a crushing blow to hear it stated with such finality.

It brings back my discussion with Karis, who has remained silent through all this. I don't blame her. I was an absolute asshole to her and said things that were hurtful that will need some serious apologizing to rectify.

For Karis, I want to be that man for her. That is, if she gives me another chance to try and prove myself. So far, I haven't scored on that penalty.

"I can't say it's not disappointing," I say, my voice softens with agreement. "I know you are all acting in my best interests and I appreciate that. Thank you."

The EMT removes the pulse ox monitor from my finger and slides the banded oxygen mask fully off my head, then gives me a thumbs-up.

"Hey, it looks like I'm just about done here and can get a ride home from Ax." I lift my brows at him standing by his car and he gives me a wave. "But Karis, if you wouldn't mind, can I speak with you privately?"

She's quiet for a moment but then speaks up. "I'm glad to hear you're okay, Ballas, and that you don't need to go to the hospital. I can make time first thing tomorrow morning if you'd like to come by."

I accept the invitation but decide tomorrow is far too long to wait. As soon as I'm given the all-clear and a now very sober Axlerod drops me off at home, I'll be calling an Uber to take me to her place.

Technically, it *is* after midnight, so by definition it is in fact tomorrow morning.

And what I need to tell her is best done in the privacy of her home, not at the office.

31

K aris

I'm sitting cross-legged on my couch and sifting through work emails, player updates, and stats to the background noise of late-night news.

The minute I got home after the game tonight, I kicked off my shoes, changed into leggings and a cropped T-shirt, and tied my hair up into a messy bun at the top of my head.

That hairdo has gotten a whole lot messier from all the tugging and pulling I did when Coach Thomas called me about Ballas's incident.

I was so afraid something like this would happen and worried that his pride would land him in this type of situation. But I couldn't force him. He's a big boy and it's his life and career.

But it doesn't mean I haven't thought about him endlessly. It's been weeks since he stormed out of my office. I licked my wounds and waited for him to decide the direction he wanted to take. I buried myself in my work to stop myself from calling or texting.

Ballas is a smart man with nearly two decades of experience in his professional career. I have no doubt that he'll come to the right conclusion.

Unfortunately, this latest incident is probably the nail in the proverbial coffin. The choice for him to continue playing is now likely out of his hands. If he doesn't call it, then the team will be forced to keep him on the long-term injured reserve list and put him on waivers. Retirement would look a whole lot better than a man of his skills being sent back down to the AHL affiliate.

I stretch my arms over head and yawn, standing up from the couch when I notice the clock reads after twelve-thirty. Knowing Ballas wants to meet first thing tomorrow morning, I should get some sleep in preparation for whatever that discussion will bring.

My phone screen suddenly lights up and my building security app pops open with a video of someone requesting entrance. I can only see the back of a baseball cap, their face turned away from the screen. It's probably some drunk person with the wrong apartment number.

I'm about to call down to security when the man turns around and his face comes into view.

Ballas.

What the hell is he doing here?

I click the speaker button. "Ballas?"

He clears his throat. "I'm sorry I'm here so late, but there's something I need to say to you."

I shift from one bare foot to another. "Yeah? What's that?"

An amused smile forms on his lips. "Do you really want me to say it from your sidewalk?"

"It depends on what it is."

"Karis...let me in, please and I'll tell you." He holds up a bag of Skittles in front of the camera. "I'll make it worth your while."

I laugh and consider for only a moment telling him to go away. "Hmm...I suppose it wouldn't hurt."

Not too bad, I hope.

I buzz him in and then quickly hustle around to put away the work I left out on my coffee table. I'm not wearing much outside of pj's but there's no time to do anything about it, so I just do a quick check of my hair in the hallway mirror.

My reflection startles me.

I'm a mess. Makeup free with disheveled hair and the bags under my eyes look like bowling balls. If I had time, I'd run into the bathroom to at least brush my teeth. But none of that matters because the door buzzes again.

I suppose it serves him right. If he's going to show up at my doorstep in the wee hours of the morning, he's going to see me looking like this. I swing the door open and gasp.

Not only does Ballas have an egg-sized bruised lump on his forehead, but there's a bloodstain on his shirt.

"Good heavens. I hope the other guy looks better than you." I yank at his arm and pull him into the entry way, then close and lock the door again.

I spin around, about to give him the riot act, only to find he's not even there. He's walking through the living room, past the pool table, and toward the stocked bar.

"Ballas, what are you doing?"

"I need a drink," he states as he pours a whisky into a lowball glass next to the decanter. "Want one?"

Padding toward him, I place my hands on my hips.

"The last thing you should be doing is drinking more tonight," I preach, cringing at how sanctimonious I sound. He whirls around, his eyes full of amusement.

"After the week I've had, and what I plan to say to you, I need this." He knocks it back and sets the empty glass back on the table.

I walk over to the couch and plop down on the corner, folding my legs under my butt as I sit.

"Okay, you've had your drink. It's late, so let's hear it. Otherwise, I'm heading to bed. I'm scheduled to meet early tomorrow with an extremely bull-headed man. You might know him."

He snickers as he takes in what I'm wearing. Or rather, not wearing. His eyes darken as the sweep over my breasts, and I cross my arms just to spite him, but it doesn't stop the thread of awareness that spreads through my body.

Without any further discussion, Ballas looks me directly in the eyes and begins to explain his unannounced visit.

"Karis, I was wrong." His features soften with the apology. "I'm sorry I am such an idiot and an asshole."

I expel a shaky puff of air from my lungs. This man—this tough, growly, proud man—is standing before me to offer me his sincere apology. It couldn't be better even if he got down on his knees and begged for my forgiveness.

Then, to my utter surprise, he does just that.

In three long strides, he's in front of me and kneels so he's at my level, his gorgeous gray eyes swimming with sincerity.

Ballas takes my hands and holds them lightly in his.

My heart lurches in my chest and my stomach flips cartwheels from his touch.

"Can you be more specific? That's kind of an everyday occurrence." I give him a teasing smile and he huffs out a laugh.

"I deserve that." His mouth tips into a sideways grin, and he stares at me from under dark lashes. Pushing up from his knees with a small groan, he takes a seat next to me on the couch.

"Before you, I never thought a lot about my life post-hockey. I've lived in the present and ignored the inevitable future. I got scared seeing my former teammates retire season after season. They seemed lost and without purpose. I didn't want that to be me."

I tilt my head, giving him a soft smile. "It doesn't have to be..." I start, but Ballas places a finger over my lips.

"I know that now. But until recently, I was shortsighted. I believed all I had to offer to the game was my ability to play.

I was a beast on skates and never considered I could be or do anything else."

A tear gathers at the corner of my eye and I swipe it away as I nod for him to continue. I've never heard Ballas speak this openly before about his feelings. The fact that he's doing it now makes my chest want to burst open with mad respect for him and appreciation.

"Hearing you say this makes me so happy, Ballas. I was hoping—"

He shakes his head. "Not yet. I'm still not sure I'm ready to take on what you're offering. It's gonna take me a while to adjust to fully accept not playing any longer. Hockey has always been my dream, my only dream. Changing from that will be difficult."

"I know. It's hard. But we all grow with time and experience. Our dreams can change along with us," I offer. I take a moment to run my palm over his cheek, capturing a wave of his shaggy hair and tucking it behind his ear. "They don't have to just end as we age."

Ballas snorts. "Jesus, you make me sound like I'm a decrepit old man."

I lift one shoulder. "If the skate fits…"

"Ohhh, is that how it is? You deserve a spanking for that one." He snorts and makes to tackle me against the cushions, but then stops short and straightens back up to continue our discussion.

"Don't pin your hopes on me just yet, Karis," he warns, one palm held up, and my heart sinks to my feet.

I want nothing more than to see him step into the GM position and make it his own. With Ballas in that role, I would feel confident that the organization will get what it needs and let go of the reins a bit more.

"So, here's the deal…"

I'm not sure I'm going to like where this is going. I cast my eyes at his hands as it places them over mine, not wanting to face the pain his rejection will cause.

"If you haven't filled the GM role yet, I'll accept it on a temporary basis through the end of this season only. But there's a condition."

Startled that there's acceptance, I blink up at him. "More money?"

He smirks. "Nope."

"What, then?"

Ballas slides both hands over my cheeks, dragging me closer to his mouth. "I want to have time with my girlfriend. She's my number one priority."

My head snaps back and my eyes widen. "Your…girlfriend?"

"Yeah. This gorgeous, smart and sexy woman who has turned my life upside down and managed to prove to me just how wrong I've been about everything."

I hum. "Maybe not *everything*."

His thumb traces lightly over my cheek and comes to rest on my lower lip.

"I can't promise I won't make mistakes—both professionally and personally."

"Welcome to the club. I've made so many along the way, Ballas. But Marv always said that mistakes are proof we are trying. It's how we grow and learn."

He rolls his eyes. "Well, I'll be learning a lot from you, then. But there's one thing I might really suck at...and will absolutely need help with."

"What's that?" I ask, my brows knitting together in confusion.

With the speed of a leopard, he pounces on me, pinning his body against mine, his palms pressed into the couch cushion to hold his chest above mine.

"I may need to fuck your brains out every time we're in a meeting together, and that could be a problem."

I giggle. "That's kind of how I feel about you all the time these days. I always worry everyone is going to see how attracted I am to you."

Leaning his head down, he gives me a long, meaningful look, his gaze searching mine as if he's lost something in them. Under the weight of his deep, penetrating stare and the delicious flex of his hips, shivers topple down my back.

I curl my fingers behind his neck and the edge of his hair dusts over my knuckles.

"Karis, I've never been in love with a woman before."

Oh boy. Here we go. This is his way of reminding me that he doesn't want anything serious, just sex.

Can I handle that? I won't keep our affair secret any longer and it will become public knowledge soon. Could I get through each day knowing he might want to move on to another woman at any time?

I guess I'll just have to work on that, just as I have everything else in my life. It's one step and one day at a time. But if you want something bad enough, you'll do anything to have it.

And I want Ballas.

My response is barely a whisper. "I know."

"But I've fallen for you."

His words rock my core.

"You...*what* now?"

My surprised reaction is stolen from my lips when he dips his head and seals his mouth over mine, kissing me deeply for the first time in weeks. The moment our lips meet, fireworks go off low in my belly. My fingers dig into his nape and I pull him closer to return his kiss hard, giving him everything I have and all that I am.

When we're out of breath, he finally pushes away, his mouth wet and thoroughly kissed.

"I love you, Karis. And I want this with you. If you'll give me the chance to prove I can be the man you need."

I stare up into his eyes and see our past, present and future reflected in them.

"Ballas, you've been the man for me since our first night together in Vegas."

He gives me that sexy, crooked grin of his and angles his hips so his thickening erection dips between my legs.

Ballas's voice turns gruff, triggering a visceral heat at my core. His eyes linger on my face for a beat.

"I'm going to continue proving that to you every day from now on."

"Starting now?" I ask, hooking my ankles behind his back and gasping when he swings me up into his arms and stands with a deep groan and I giggle.

"We better start now because we both know I'm not getting any younger."

EPILOGUE

April - Six Months Later

"The car is here," Ballas says softly, his hand placed gently against the small of my back. "You ready to head over to the reception?"

I stare out at the green rolling hills blanketed with the first signs of spring and think about all the changes that occurred in my life this past year.

The last year and a half has taught me lessons about the strength I possess I never knew I had. That I am as resilient as I am vulnerable, and it's the hard lessons that led me to making difficult decisions, like the one I had to make about Marv.

This will go down in history as the most difficult week of my life. It could've had me curled up in a little ball on the bathroom floor, sobbing fits of tears. Instead, I grieved and got through it with the most incredible man by my side.

Five days ago, I said goodbye to the one person who kept me going for so long when I was young and had lost everything. I finally let Marv go after a series of infections he battled valiantly brought his life to an end. He passed comfortably in his bed, surrounded by those who cared about him.

Ballas, ever the stoic and strong one, wrapped me in his unrelenting arms and held me tight throughout, reminding me that with love, you can endure anything, no matter how painful.

The grieving process continued in a different format when I signed the contracts to sell the Puget Sound Pilots. As if Marv himself was giving me permission to let go, all the chips landed perfectly for a complicated but very lucrative deal for me to hand the franchise over to a new ownership group.

I'd been working on it for months after finally reaching the tough decision that I didn't have the bandwidth to own two professional sports teams, manage several business holdings, and have any sort of personal life.

With Ballas now permanently in the role of the Vikings general manager, as well as my committed boyfriend, I didn't want to split my time into tiny slivers between Seattle and Vancouver. The Pilots and the Vikings.

Thankfully, I know my Pilots team will be in good hands because the new ownership group includes Marek and Harper Talbert. I couldn't be happier about this shift and what it means for the team's future and the future of their family.

I slip my gloved hand through Ballas's, turning back one more time to say my silent goodbyes to Marv and my parents, who are all now buried side by side in the family plot. Ballas places a kiss on the top of my head and leads me to the black SUV waiting to take us to where a reception is being hosted for Marv.

As we get settled in the back of the car, I lean into Ballas's chest, his arm wrapped around my shoulder, and breathe in his smoky, woodsy scent.

"You sure you want to do this?" he asks, pushing a lock of hair that's come loose behind my ear. "I can take you back to the house if you don't want a crowd, make you forget all your sorrows."

He gives me a gentle smile, his eyes crinkling with sweet mischief, and I poke him in the ribs. "I can't believe you're thinking about sex right now."

He shrugs against me. "What? I'm just being a loving, supporting partner. Isn't that what I should do?"

Giggling, I press my cheek back to his chest. Ballas has claimed that role in spades and claimed my heart in the process. I couldn't have asked for a better partner. I've been through so much since our first hookup in Vegas; going through a break up with a cheating ex, dealing with my uncle's life-altering medical event and subsequent coma, assuming responsibility of Marv's businesses and two professional teams and then falling in love with a veteran hockey player.

And now making the huge decision to let my uncle go in peace.

I may be stronger than I thought, but it's impossible to

believe I could've ever managed all of this on my own without my beast of a man—and his big heart—by my side.

That's what love does for you. It gives you an assist when you face off against life's biggest challenges.

Ballas may not play professional hockey any longer, but he's my player for life.

The End

AFTERWORD

Thank you so much for reading book #1 in the new Vancouver Vikings Hockey series. I hope you enjoyed the start of this new series. I can't wait to share with you all the new players who will be featured in upcoming books, including:

Off the Stick - Book #2 (Dane "Ax" Axlerod and Halle MacAlister)

Off the Post - Book #3 (Soren Wolfenspiel)

Off the Bench - Book #4 (Shaw Benning)

Off the Ice - Book #5 (Gunnar Svensson)

If you enjoyed this book, I'd greatly appreciate a review on any of the platforms where you post. Thank you!

ACKNOWLEDGMENTS

A huge thank you to my PA and Gal Friday, Melissa, who is always so fun and enthusiastic and such a delight to work with. Your support is invaluable to me.

To my agent at SBR Media. I am so grateful to you for all you've done for me so far. You work tirelessly to ensure your clients have all the best opportunities in publishing. Thank you for your support.

To my editor, Sandy, the HOCKEY guru! Her insight and expertise in the game, as well as her attention to detail, were a lifesaver to me as I rewrote this story. Thank you so much!

To my Seattle Kraken players...I watched. I learned. I swooned. Thanks for being such an awesome team of players and getting me back into the game of hockey.

ABOUT THE AUTHOR

Sierra Hill is a *2020 RONE Award-Winning* author of **Game Changer**, as well as over 50 novels, including the award-winning college sports series, **Courting Love**, and the twice award-finalist erotic ménage serial, **Reckless – The Smoky Mountain Trio**.

Subscribe to her email list and download a FREE book here: www.sierrahillbooks.com

And don't forget to look for me on one of these socials:

MORE SPORTS ROMANCE FROM SIERRA HILL

Hockey

Vancouver Vikings Hockey

Offside (A Vancouver Vikings Series Book #1)

Off the Stick (A Vancouver Vikings Series Book #2)

Off the Post (A Vancouver Vikings Series - Book #3)

Playmaker (A World of True North Moo U novel)

The Hockey Player and the Tutor

The Puget Sound Pilots (Sports Romance)

The Girlfriend Game (Book #1)

The Wife Win (Book #2)

The Rival Romeo (Book #3)

Change of Hearts (A College Campus Series)

Game Changer (Book #1)

Change in Strategy (Book #2)

Change of Course (Book #3)

Courting Love (College Sports)

Full Court Press

The Rebound

Pivot

Fast Break

Jump Shot

www.ingramcontent.com/pod-product-compliance
Lightning Source LLC
Chambersburg PA
CBHW070450300726
48975CB00007B/2114